The May Anthology
of Oxford and Cambridge Short Stories 1999

Varsity/Cherwell

First published in 1999 by Varsity Publications Ltd

ISBN: 0 902240 27 7

A CIP catalogue record for this book is available from the British Library.

Typeset by Suzanne Arnold
Produced by Origen Production Limited
Printed and bound in Great Britain

Original concept: Peter Davies, Adrian Woolfson, Ron Dimant

Further copies of this book are available from good bookshops in Cambridge and Oxford, or direct from Varsity Publications Ltd, 11-12 Trumpington Street, Cambridge, CB2 1QA

Editors: Sophie Craig, Benjamin Yeoh (Cambridge)
Chris Tryhorn, Matt Edwards (Oxford)

Executive Editor: Penelope Lively

Publisher: Suzanne Arnold

Cover Design: Alex Evans, Benjamin Yeoh

Cover Photos: Benjamin Yeoh

Editorial Committee: Rowland Byass, Ruth Fowler, Felicity
Howlett, Nick Hayman-Joyce, Michelle LeLievre, Laura Phillips,
Susan Thomas, Naomi West, Gerhardt Will

Cambridge College Sponsors: Churchill, Clare, Corpus Christi,
Darwin, Fitzwilliam, Gonville & Caius, Kings', Jesus, Pembroke,
Robinson, Queens', Sidney Sussex, Trinity

Oxford College Sponsors: New College, St Anne's, St Hugh's,
St John's, Templeton, Wadham, Wolfson

Thank you also to Carole Blake, Penguin Press, Hodder Headline,
Dr Michael Franklin, Rachel Flowerday, Alex von Tunzelmann
for their assistance

Contents

Introduction   9

Afrique   Richard Antwi   11

House Call   Jay Basu   29

Heart's Desire   Heather Clark   39

The Gift of TV   Katharine Edgar   53

The Descent of   Laura James   77
Dr Campbell

Mrs Perkins' Anatomy   Anna Khoo   91

Fortune's Goose   David McCallam   101

The Ascension of   Hillary Stevens   115
the Beasts

The Coffee Habit   Katharine Whitfield   145

Notes on Contributors   165

Introduction

There was a gratifying diversity to the stories submitted. And also a welcome absence of obvious influences. Influence is both inevitable and fruitful, but it can also have a heavy hand. So it was good to read a clutch of stories which did not sing out their particular placing in time and space. Several had a distinctly timeless quality; others could not have been written at any point but the late twentieth century but were not slavishly contemporary. There was a nice mix of realism and fantasy, too – with fantasy sometimes having the edge as in a favourite of mine, *The Descent of Dr Campbell*, which triumphantly tackled the problem of what to write a short story about and how to give it individuality.

This is pertinent, because to my mind the short story is a fiendishly difficult form. Pretty well anyone could write one – of a sort. Few can turn out something that seizes the reader's attention in terms of both subject and style. The only reason that the story seems a suitable form for cutting one's literary teeth on is that it is short. In many ways it is easier to write a novel. And there is always the insidious urge to tell a story in the first person, which is quite the most taxing and treacherous narrative mode going. The writers here who chose that voice got away with it, on the whole. But its lure is an aspect of the deceptive quality of the short story. Surely story-telling comes naturally, we say to ourselves. Not so at all; nothing is more artful.

PENELOPE LIVELY
March 1999

Afrique

Part I
Gold Coast, West Africa, Early-Nineteenth Century.

Edward tried again. Putting the pocket watch back and gripping his cane with his left hand, he paused and then attempted the manoeuvre in one movement. Sharply, he slid his right hand into his pocket, produced the watch and fumbled with the catch to open it. He succeeded on his third attempt, the pleasure making him smile. He had often watched the white men at port. Occasionally they would flick open their pocket watches with an ease which left Edward in awe: the authority of it! Now he could do it and the pride he felt numbed the pain of his long walk to the colony.

He studied the watch given to him by his chief. He had learnt how to flick it and how to look at it, but what in particular he was supposed to look for remained a mystery. It was just covered in lines but nothing ever happened. "If it is important for them, then it is important for me," he assured himself, continuing his practice as he strolled. He stopped occasionally to take the stones which cut him out of his shoes. Their state matched the worn, sun-bleached suit, given to him by a man at port for his services. As he walked he wondered how he could get a white chest cloth, like that of the governor.

The trees on either side of the track blocked his vision as he scoured the sky for the sun. Moving closer to the edge of the dirt road, he grappled with the foliage. The sun had just left the horizon, he had plenty of time. Re-centring

11

himself, he continued his journey. He walked majestically, proud in his stride as he continued his practice. He could not wait to impress the men at port.

He looked about him, at the grand trees, splendid in variety, their flowers in full blossom, curvaceous, exuding a soporific sweetness, their branches towering over the road. He loved to walk down this road. Loved to taste the smell of seasoned fruits, generously giving their fragrance to the warm morning air. To see the great mahoganies, so prized in the port. The rhythmic clicking of his practice was only overshadowed by the shrills of the birds. It sounded as if they were mocking him, he thought to himself, asking how he could go to work on such a day.

He stopped walking sharply, startled by a common sound in an uncommon place. It was a drone, a faint singing, a man's voice, approaching, coming around the bend in the road. Deftly he closed the watch and slipped it into his pocket, haste perfecting his practice. Edward brushed his hands on his clothes and resumed his walk with a renewed pomp as the figure approached. "Nana, what brings you out so early on this morning?" he said, greeting his neighbour. Edward knew Nana very well, but of late they had grown apart.

"Brother Kofi," began Nana, drawing a long breath, feeling the vapours of the liquor in his stomach warming his insides. "It was the pleasures of the night which brought me out, this morning only returns me." The liquor grinned in his face, broadly.

"Where have you been all night?" enquired Edward who was becoming agitated by his friend's state.

"To the christening of Mother Akua's child. It is not often that one witnesses such a rich display. Everyone attended. Even those from Nzema made the journey. Your absence…" He paused. "Was profoundly missed." Nana felt the tingling sensation of the liquor gradually leaving his body as he spoke, he felt himself becoming more sober. He felt more aware of his surroundings, the activity about him, the change in Edward's manner, who was somewhat taken aback, his mind foraging for some explanation.

"Yes…well…I did not know of the occasion…w…with work and all my time is…" his search, now desperate, disrupted his speech, "I didn't know."

Nana decided not to mention the fact that Edward's wife was there, realising how raw the nerve that he touched was. Instead he changed the subject: "Where are you going?"

"To work," the words gushed from his mouth as he addressed the world. "I work in the colony, with the white men, the Europeans." Edward produced a piece of cloth from his trouser waist. The sun shone brightly, reflecting the Kente pattern. "They pay me." He untied it and showed Nana the round pieces of metal. He stooped forward, arms outstretched so Nana could get a better look but kept it just out of reach. "I have people under my charge, everyone knows me. You must come and visit me, just ask for Edward."

"Edward." Nana repeated the strange word back to him.

"The governor calls me Edward, like a son of his own, his surname is Edward." The pride straightened his shoulders as he spoke. He carefully tied the coins up in their protective cloth and tucked it back into his waist.

Nana felt the disgust rising from his chest but it stopped in his throat, stifled by the sheer comedy of it all. He let out a short burst of air through his nose as he smiled. Lowering

13

his head, he stalked around Edward, and walked towards a tree. It was a great mahogany, as old as the land in which it grew. Its trunk had been split down the centre by lightning and the people cherished it like an ancestral tree. The tree stood like a monument of the rich country and the life it nurtured. The mahogany held a memory for every person who had received shelter from the afternoon rains. On any summer's evening, one was sure to hear a mother telling the children a story about the power of the tree. It wore its age nobly, some of its branches were as thick as the trunks of its kin and its canopy was high above the rest. The shadows it cast crept from the west in the morning and to the east they went each night.

Nana looked at the sun rising between the fork in the tree's trunk. He ran his hands along the bark, noticing a snail on the other side, creeping towards the tree. He turned to face Edward who was standing, quite bewildered by Nana's behaviour. Nana looked down at his feet and traced the shadows away from himself to where they stopped; his eyes rested on Edward's feet. He traced his attire, up, up, looking at the boy he played with, grew up with, and tried to reconcile the child with the man. He looked at the blazer, barely held together by its remaining thread, soaking up the sweat from his chest, still unable to think. He traced the familiar face, the full mouth, his unusually straight nose and those eyes which he had seen cry, laugh, think and die; for it was a different man he saw now. The injustice of it all. There he stopped, staring, and his emotions spoke.

"Do you remember when we used to play in this tree," – Nana hoped that in rekindling Edward's childhood, memories, he might rekindle his smouldering spirit – "all those years ago?" As he spoke he caressed the bark behind his lower back, mapping its ridges with his fingers. He talked with a removed expression, his heart in his voice but his mind somewhere else. "How we used to climb up into its shelter and look out east, over the lands of the Anlo people and west to the people of Wassa. They say the world will end when the sun crosses this tree from north to south."

Edward stood surprised by the whole situation. 'What had brought it about?' he thought. He found a tongue to reply. "Yes, I remember. I remember." Edward said softly, then he erupted. "Do you know the men at port…?"

"The white men?" Nana interrupted, clarifying the subject matter. Edward sensed the animosity and began again, less enthusiastic.

"Yes," he said softly, more to himself than to his stubborn audience. "Yes, the white men. The white men at port. They also have a joke like yours, they say: 'The price of slaves rises with the sun and the price of ivory sets with it.'" Edward followed his joke with a laugh. He knew it was appropriate too.

Nana listened, dumbfounded. "Kofi, your learning confuses me, please explain." Edward's pleasure at being asked to elucidate personified itself. With shoulders back and leaning on his cane, he savoured the moment, prolonging his importance.

"Well at the port they say that slaves…" He struggled to remember how it had been explained to him. "Slaves are more money, you get more money for slaves…their price is rising, yes rising." At this point he flicked open the watch and held it out, to the world. His speech began to flow. "The original Slave Coast was in the east and the sun rises in the east. The Ivory Coast is in the?" He slowed his speech and answered his question. "West," he said,

15

extending the syllables like a person helping another to learn a language, or a teacher taking her children through the alphabet, stressing the importance of every single letter. "The price of ivory is going down like the sun does." His explanation ended with the now customary laughter.

Nana had stopped listening to him a long time ago. The sun was beginning to give its full heat. He felt his head and neck heating up. He watched the snail creeping beneath a leaf to avoid drying up. He felt the sensation one feels before crying, around his eyes, mouth and in his chest. His cry was inspired by sorrow, a sorrow induced by anger. "So you work in the fort now." Edward shielded his eyes with the cane still in his hand, holding it in the air.

"Yes, I have many friends there. The fort is a magnificent place. Larger than any village. The governor's house is larger than that of any chief and dyed white. There are fifty different levels and thousands of rooms, all decorated in the oldest mahogany. Heavy cloths of gold thread hang on all the walls. The governor lives inside this house. I've seen him." As he finished speaking he swiftly put the pocket watch back.

Nana just observed him all the while. He even allowed himself to grin. Edward continued, "Tomorrow I am going on a raid, expedition. To capture slaves, villagers. The captain tells me that with a lot more work…" Nana did not let him finish.

"To capture who? Villagers? Kofi my brother, you, like me, are a 'villager'. You were born in a village, grew up in a village and still live in a village and you talk of villagers? Who exactly are you going to capture, your mother, wife, kids?" Nana said, maintaining his quietude.

"I work with the Europeans, I dress smartly and that is my work." He flicked the watch as if to reinforce his point. "You could never dress like this. Have you seen a villager who can? My friend, indeed I am distinct. You could never dress like me." Edward was irritated by now. The fierce sun adding to his anger, making him feel uncomfortable.

"And my brother," Nana paused. "I could never know the bins of the governor like you," retorted Nana, all respect gone.

"What do you mean? The governor's bins? Bins! My friend, look at you and me. Who knows bins? I am not the poor farmer. I move up with every day which passes. As I was saying before," his tone calm again, "with a lot more work… the captain says I will be rich, as he. So who are you to lecture me bush boy?"

Nana felt the breath rush from him, his spine arched backwards, his mouth agape. The noise swept the birds from the canopy. The laughter tore at his insides and ripped the humid morning. Then it stopped, as abruptly as it began. The spasms ceased, the warmth of laughter absorbed in the heat of anger. He stood tall, broad, droplets of sweat catching each other, scurrying down his spine. Edward noticed how big and muscular Nana was. He could feel Nana's eyes burning on his skin. The sun was rising high, he wanted to be on his way. To leave Nana and his ignorance in the bush.

Nana kept his eyes on Edward as he slowly reached up and locked his hands onto a branch. Then slowly, like the movement of a sloth, strong, taut, he pulled himself up. Sweat rolled by the co-ordination of his muscles, soaked his shorts. Up he moved, twisting, pulling, turning, controlled. All traces of his stupor gone, moving as surely as if he was one with the tree. He brought himself to rest in the fork of the trunk and looked down, at Edward, who stood baffled, intimidated by the silhouette in the tree.

"Kofi" – Nana spoke – "Rich. You want to be rich. What is rich? What do your coins buy in the village? Where do you spend your money? What do you have that everyone can't grow, can't make, for the price of work? Brother," he almost cried the word, "you had hardships like I, but you were never poor."

"I was not poor," Edward said in disbelief. "I did not have the riches of the chief."

"And what have you now, European cloths and coins you cannot spend? Kofi, you are at the bottom of his tribe," reasoned Nana.

"What difference does it make? Is there not a hierarchy in the village? What is the chief? Look at his house, his family, his kids! I'm getting paid for being at this bottom!"

Nana raised his voice. "Were you not allowed to approach the chief? When your crops failed, was it not his house your family was fed at? Were your problems not his, his joy yours? You talk of his kids, did your children not play freely with his? Don't they regard one another as brother and sister? They swim together, cry together, dance together, sleep together." He rose out of his seat as he spoke, casting an ominous shadow. "You serve those men, you can't enter his house, you hang … hover on the porch with the mosquitoes. While he passes messages through one privileged enough. Your kids serve his kids, they are being taught their place. Kofi, tame a puppy, teach it its place and the dog will never bark at you."

"Shut up," screamed Edward, waving his cane at the

figure in the tree. Rebuking the onslaught. "Go and tend your yams, bush idiot!"

"Why are you carrying that stick?" Edward dropped the stick as the question was asked and stumbled back. "You talk and talk 'the port', 'the Europeans', 'the white men', the white men," mimicked Nana. "Empty bellows make a lot of noise. Before they came and sat on your people, you did not know poverty. Yet it has infected you like the flu. You know no cure. They brought the disease and no cure! Your mind is sick and your body is suffering, you are spending your life trying to rid yourself of poverty. Your searching feeds it, breeds it…poor man…fool."

Edward was motionless, transfixed by the black figure which stood in the tree, outlined by the sun approaching its apex. The shadow cast by the figure was all over him. He felt the hand of fear run its finger down his spine. He took a step back; the figure remained still, upright. Edward could feel his nose running and for some reason, his body was shaking. As he turned he stumbled on his shoes, feeling the coarse dirt from the road on his face. He jumped up, disorientated, almost in a frenetic state, he couldn't take his eyes off the figure in the tree, too afraid to turn away. He continued fumbling, scrambling down the road to get away, seeking safety, the safety of the port.

The further Edward got, the higher Nana climbed, not allowing him to evade his shadow. In a last bout of confidence Edward turned and screamed: "The name's Edward, not Kofi. Edward, bush idiot. You'll see…I will show you who I…" his voice drifted off and he was gone, around the bend. The only remnants of his presence were a stick, broken from some tree and the distant sound of a man, running.

Nana waited until the man was gone and allowed himself to chuckle. He had never known such a stupid man. He climbed down and picked up the stick Edward had once wielded. It was the hottest part of the day and he noticed that the snail was feeding in the canopy of the tree, hidden from the sun's glare. "Edward." He repeated the name to himself and laughed as he began his journey home. He took a fruit out of his pocket, happy he had taken it for the long walk home. He smelled it to confirm the orange, reds and yellows of its skin. The sticky nectar ran down his throat and dripped onto his chest, as he sucked the stringy pith. He tapped a beat with the stick, then tossed it behind him and began to hum his song, musing on the story he had to tell.

Part II

The night was hot, very humid and the village was virtually asleep, apart from the odd murmur and the aura of a group of lanterns in the distance, swaying as they approached. Nana lay back and tilted the clay bowl against his lips, letting the palm wine trickle down his throat as he recounted the day's events. He had told all to his wife, who had laughed more than he did. He smiled at the thought of her laughing face and could taste the palmoil from his meal as he ran his tongue around his mouth. Listening to the sounds of the children being put to bed, he wondered what tomorrow would bring.

Finally, the fulsome figure of his wife entered. His stomach fluttered at her beauty. She was one of the prettiest ladies in the village and Nana felt that familiar stirring.

"Come," was all he said, beckoning her with his hand. She slipped off her cloth and approached the mat on which he lay. Her beauty seemed ephemeral, he thought to himself, special to this night and he was eager to live the moment.

She lay beside him. The lanterns had stopped approaching and were now illuminating the tiny hut. They kissed, softly. Slow, soft kisses. There was a fervent whispering outside, questions being asked, then came a silence. She lay her leg over his, caressing his calf, arms intertwined, searching. A man peered through the doorway and darted his head back out. "Y…yes," he said, giving confirmation to the party who hovered outside.

Mindlessly they stormed in. It was a wrecking frenzy, tables, stools, smashed; precious ornaments broken; heirlooms, heritage, culture, history, destroyed. The screaming of the children woke Nana from his surprise. In vain he tried to defend his home from the six houseslaves and the four white men. A large man grabbed him as a white man punched him, but they had underestimated the strength of Nana. He fought back, viciously. Breaking away from his captor, he pounded the face of the houseslave before they gripped him again. This time it was two slaves. The cries of his wife amplified the children's screams. "Against your own," she yelled repeatedly, but they didn't hear as they beat Nana. "Bastards…STOP IT…NO, against your brother. If he was white would you strike him? Uh." She pleaded for an answer in her screams.

She grasped the two children close to her, pressing one face into her thigh and the other into her hip, shielding them from the horror, muffling their cries whilst voicing her own. Tears fell down her face as they punched and

21

kicked Nana in turn. He fought on, pushing, kicking, scratching, lashing out. He was overpowered and knew to himself that he could not go on for long. She watched the father of her children through her tears. "No," she cried as she let go of her children. She reached across the wall, feeling for Nana's hunting blade. Her heart pounded in her head as she hissed a deep breath through her teeth. "No." She screamed running towards the pack, arms aloft, blade unsheathed.

The distance was too far. Her screams were passionate but served to alert the pack. One of the fortune seekers turned and looked at the wild African woman running towards him. He was drenched in sweat and the blood of Nana. His stubby hands slowly clenched into fists. He watched her run, he saw the knife and let out a very low content laugh. Nana yelled for her to stop but was silenced by a blow to his mouth. There was a symphony of noise as his fist connected square on with her face. It began with the owner of the fist grunting his satisfaction. Then came the multiple screams of the children and Nana, ending with the sound of a head hitting the floor; she was out cold. The white man stepped back, admiring his work, his arm still in its position of impact. His companions burst into laughter, the houseslaves stood silent, fear and surprise pumping in their veins. Nana stopped struggling and sank into captivity. A tear rolled down his face.

'Crack' thundered the governor's cane against a fragment of mirror as he entered. His very steps and posture exaggerated, like a fighting cock strutting before a foe. He was in his mid-forties. An average specimen of the privileged sector of British society, he had joined the Merchant Trading Company soon after leaving Oxford, to escape joining the army, his father and to make his fortune. He rapidly ascended through the ranks and here he was, Governor, somehow persuaded to sort out a petty African altercation. Days like this provided some animation to the mundane trade. He was tiring of the idiocy of the niggers and would have returned to his lush lawns in England had his manor house been completed. Besides, being in Africa did have its benefits. There was no shortage of women in port who could provide services like the ladies of Piccadilly, only for nothing, with persuasion. Edward hobbled in after him and stopped in the doorway.

The governor continued his walk. He had never been inside the house of a native and felt his youthful curiosity awakening. He walked past the men who now held the placid Nana. His eyes studied the gold ornaments, trinkets and various blades, paraphernalia which lay strewn. He stepped over the body of Nana's wife and strolled around the living quarters. He looked at the matting and the cloths strewn across the floor. He studied the muscular figures of the tiny children, who held each other tightly. His eyes wandered to a bowl of white liquid at their feet. He picked it up and smelled it, swirled it around and walked back over to others who were all watching him, awaiting instruction. "Drink," the governor mouthed to Nana whilst making drinking motions. He understood and nodded his reply. The governor, not taking his eyes off Nana, took a mouthful and washed it around his mouth. It tasted sweet yet had a bitterness to it, like any good palm wine.

Nana winced as the wine was spat back into his face. He felt it entering the cuts, stinging, the white nectar sinking slowly into his hair, running down his face. "Hardly port is it!" The quip was followed by a raucous bout of laughter

23

from the white men. The houseslaves looked at each other and they laughed also, timing their end to coincide with the whites. The children began to cry. Nothing was funny for them.

"Edward," bellowed the governor. Edward crept forth from the shadow of the doorway, hunched over, clasping his hands.

"Y…yes sa."

"Is this the man who tried to kill you?" Nana raised his eyes to look at his jury, his judge and then he fixed his eyes on the plaintiff. Edward darted his eyes to the ground.

"Y…y…yes sa," he mumbled.

"Speak up. Is it or isn't it?" His patience was wearing thin. Edward raised his head, realising that he had the advantage now. He stood upright and faced Nana. His eyebrows made a 'v' as he sneered.

"Yes," he said clearly. Nana did not react.

"Yes who?" Sneered the governor, only speaking through half of his mouth.

"Y…yes…s…sa," Edward muttered.

Nana tilted his head back and laughed, thin lines of palm wine, sweat and blood rolling into his mouth. "Fool," he said to Edward in Twi. Nana knew very little English, but Edward's position was clear. "Bloody…"

"Shut your thick African mouth," shouted the governor. Nana just grinned broadly. He had lost all fear; he didn't care anymore. "Take him away." The governor said as he left the room, throwing the bowl of palm wine behind him. The houseslaves gripped him and dragged their prize out of the house. The torches haloed the party. The children wiped the palm wine off their faces and clung to their mother's body, sobbing as she regained consciousness.

Nana was silent in his sorrows as he contemplated where they were taking him. He had often heard the stories of how they took people to a distant land where food and crops were plentiful, the sun always shone and life was sweet. He had been told of how they took people by the shipload but didn't know whether to believe it. They could be lies. However there must be something there, nobody hated it enough to return.

He could see Edward out of the corner of his eye approaching him rapidly. Edward spoke into his ear: "Who's the fool? You'll see I...I...w...will buy your family poor man. You will see who's a fool, you will see." His taunts were followed with his laughter.

"Kofi, I am only poor in your white mind, rich in spirit." Edward gathered the phlegm from his throat and balanced it on his lower lip. His stomach jerked as he projected it into Nana's face.

"Your juju talk will not help you now!" He laughed again with the same falseness, only this time louder.

"You may laugh but I hear your screams," Nana said. Edward missed the last remark, he was too busy trying to laugh.

The procession continued. Most of the village was now watching, women cried and yelled, some men pleaded from a distance, others kept silent. They knew the dangers of the Europeans. Some of the braver kids ran around the procession, their anxious mothers calling for them to come home.

The governor walked ahead, alone. He wondered what to do next. He never knew of the village before and he had seen some fine men who could easily be sold. He also knew from Nana's house that they had gold. He fingered a bottletop in his pocket as he thought. He would have to come back with more men and guns. To try to capture more now would mean certain death. Africans could be dangerous once provoked. Nonetheless, he knew he had to act quickly before some foreigner got their hands in first. He decided to come back during the week. His little nigger had found him a pot of gold in the jungle. He felt glad that he came along.

"Edward." The governor called out over the singing of the children.

"Y…yes sa," he answered, running up alongside him.

"Here, you have been good." The governor said as he produced the small metal disc from his pocket. A few slaves saw Edward's reward and looked on, enviously. Some of the white men smirked and carried on walking.

"T'ank you. T'ank you sa." Edward stopped walking and stepped aside, into the shrubbery beside the road, letting the procession pass him by. Nana watched him standing alone as he passed; he heard a high shrill scream and knew it was his wife.

Carefully, Edward unfolded his trouser waist and took out the Kente cloth. Cradling his treasure, he added the reward to his hoard. He lingered, savouring the sight of all his work, all of those long days and now his personal treasure of European generosity. He tied it up and folded it back into his trousers. His victory truly crowned, he grinned, smiled and then laughed. He jogged to catch up to his companions, off back to the colony, to the governor's house in port. His laughter was echoed by the voices of the children's singing; they sang:

26

Obroni, how are you?
I am fine thank you.
Obroni, how…

Note:
Obroni – Twi word meaning white man

RICHARD ANTWI

House Call

My father had taken me with him to the house in India. I was eleven years old, my mind keen to the new world I had found myself in, very different from the London streets that up until then had formed the only terrain of my imagination. I was quietly awe-struck by the grand decaying topologies of the house; the peeling cream and burgundy paintwork, dulled by an accumulation of old-age and dust from the main street outside; the vast marble floors; the dusty concrete plateau of the roof; the cool dark rooms in which my great-aunt (whom my father called 'Jethi') would recline among the shadows, smiling and ruffling my hair whenever I wandered into her view. The large house – the biggest house in the town – gave off a palpable air of faded wealth, which even as a child I could feel heavy in my eyes and lungs like perfume. It was as if the grandeur of its former life (in the days when my eleven-year-old father walked its marble corridors) lay dormant in the aging walls, waiting for some signal to spring to life once more. But although I did not know it then, the house was heavy with death. My father's mother ('Ma') had died eighteen months before from a life long affliction of diabetes, leaving my grandfather, 'Baba', along with my great-aunt and great-uncle the house's remaining occupants. Then, a few months after my grandmother's death, a cousin, Tupoon, died in odd circumstances, sending a second wave of tragedy shuddering through the family, so soon after the first. Tupoon was seventeen, a tall, lithe boy who excelled in sport at school and whose photograph – of a fluffy-haired young Indian flashing his white adamantine teeth at the lens – still sits amongst the albums at my parents' house in London. He had collapsed

29

in his college room and was rushed to P.G. Hospital in Calcutta where his skin had turned the colour of mortar and, several hours later, he had stopped breathing. When his body was opened up under the neon autopsy lights he was found to have only one kidney, which, after seventeen years of doing more than could be reasonably asked of it, had finally failed him. It seemed the most arbitrary kind of loss, and it shocked Tupoon's father, Burruda, to his core. Without a wife to share the burden of grief (she had passed away from cancer many years before) Burruda's own health radically eroded. He became an increasingly thin, wasted figure, as if his body, devoid of the dream that had sustained it, were systematically cancelling itself out. Burruda – who had been both a cousin and great childhood friend to my father – was taken into the house and attended to by the house-servants in my father's old bedroom until his body was able to complete its project. He had finally deleted himself only a few weeks before our visit.

Whilst this web of tragedy wrapped itself around the family in the Indian heat, my father was in London where he had lived for thirty years with my mother, my sister and me. When he received the telegram of Burruda's death he had decided to travel again to India. He had been there, alone, only a year and a half before to attend his mother's funeral ceremony, but now decided to take me with him (my mother, at that point a librarian at the borough library, was unable to take enough time off work). He has told me since that he was motivated not only by a desire to pay respect to his late cousin but also by an urgent need he felt to show me the part of myself that resided in India, within his family and the world which they inhabited. He suspected – and he was right – that Baba, Jethi and Jetha, as well as the house, would not last much longer, and he wanted to make sure their memory was implanted, like a diamond in ore, somewhere in his young son's mind. Why he didn't take my sister (either as well as or instead of me) was put down to lack of money and her age – she was four years my junior – but I believe now it also had much to do with the unspoken relations which flow between a father and a son on the verge of becoming a man, mingled in our case with the residue of the middle-class Indian value system where fathers rise like monoliths over their families, and their sons, in turn, continue the chain-of-command.

Whatever the reasons, I found myself a few days later in the town of Bankura, to the east of Calcutta. And as far as I was concerned it was to be a great holiday. Like a conservationist releasing a bird into the wild, my father let me gleefully soak up the undivided attentions of his family. Jethi would chat to me in Bengali (which I didn't understand) and continually send for more sweets for me to gorge myself on, ignoring the half-hearted protestations of my father. As the wealth of my father's family lessened over the years many of the thirty or so house servants could no longer be maintained, but seven or eight still remained, doing basic chores and preparing the food and the beds. To me they were a restless group of people, buzzing in and out of doorways, bringing food for us or tall glasses of water for Baba before moving away to another part of the house as quickly and silently as they had arrived. It seemed to me that these courteous flitting ghosts collectively constituted the lifeblood of the house, efficiently and unobtrusively keeping the hearts of the aged occupants beating strong, maintaining order and equilibrium always out of sight, just beneath the skin. Occasionally one of them would catch me running down a hallway or along the balcony and raise a stern palm up to my face, gently chiding my childish recklessness at risking a bad fall on the smooth marble. At certain times of the day they would congregate in the bright concrete courtyard at the back of the house where the kitchens were. Here, talking and smoking, their professional mystery would dissolve away, and if I happened into their company they would loudly chatter Bengali to me, laughing and whooping at my bewildered responses.

We stayed for three weeks. During the days I would travel with my father to visit various friends in town, otherwise I would remain in the house, amusing myself in the large, square garden which had become overgrown and dense with foliage, the elderly occupants both unable and unwilling to keep it tended. I would crouch down on the grass and watch the progress of the huge bloated ants that made their way like tiny articulated lorries along paths visible only to them. Or I would run up the marble stairs to the roof, which became a concrete horizon in which I could play unhindered inside my own head. Occasionally I would turn off before I reached the roof and hesitate by the doorway of the small silent room in which Jetha, my great-uncle, kept his paintings. Jetha had for many years been the District Judge for Bankura, and had fuelled his private life by painting portraits of Hindu Gods and Goddesses, often interpreting the 'visions' which my grandmother purported to have in moments of meditation. I had been told by my father not to touch anything in Jetha's painting place, and an air of the sacred filled the little room, seeping from the spectral faces which looked out benignly from the canvasses around the walls. In the great maze of the old house, Jetha's painting room was the only turning I could not explore.

At night I would sit drowsily on the wide balcony that ran around nearly the entire perimeter of the house. The warm darkness clung like sweat to the house and I would gaze into the night in T-shirt and shorts, listening to the sound of my father's voice as he talked for hours with the others in the yellow light of the rooms behind me. The conversations drifted up around me like music, punctuated always by the distant hum of traffic crunching the grit along Bankura's main road. I would watch my father as he walked out with Baba onto the far end of the balcony, both craning their necks a little to look down into the rustling black pit of the garden below. Baba was a slim, gaunt man, dressed always in a fraying brown lambswool jumper and white dhoti. He had a long serious face which could seem in turn severe and mournful. My father, though less lean in figure than Baba, had and still has many physical similarities to his own father, most notably a habit of clasping both hands behind his back as he walks, a gesture simultaneously imperious and casual. As Baba and his son stood side by side in the balcony light talking softly to each other – about what I never knew – their identical shadows made deep black swipes across the marble balcony floor, which, under the electric bulb-light, gained a glossed surface like that of water. They rarely made any physical contact as they stood together on those evenings (very unlike my father's relationship with me, whom he would regularly scoop up and hug with a bellow) but instead seemed to express their love through the tight gravitational attractions of a deep but undemonstrative mutual respect.

During one of the periodic evening electrical-blackouts I stood in the doorway of our bedroom and watched my father as he sat alone on the balcony outside in the pitch darkness, his head inclined slightly to one side as if listening to the sounds his thoughts made as they ran through his mind. He was remembering other evenings lost under the hot dust of the past; evenings spent with his mother, checking his watch for when he would have to

33

fetch the insulin kit, pinch a small mound of coffee brown flesh on his mother's upper arm and jab the needle in as quick as he could while she turned away, her face for an instant transformed into a child's. It was during these brief periods of 'load-shedding'-induced darkness that the memories crowded in, beckoned by the flicker of candle-light and the silence that descended over the house like mist.

In the second week my uncle (the son of Baba's sister), Shanku, came to the house. Shanku was an eye-surgeon practising at Jalpaiguri Hospital in the north of Bengal, near Darjeeling. He was a handsome man with intelligent features and a clipped black moustache which, rather than making him look older, seemed to accentuate the youthfulness of his wide face. When my father introduced him to me I had asked incredulously how anyone could perform surgery on an eye. Shanku had bent down close, fixed me in his gaze and whispered his answer conspiratorially, illustrating the words with exaggerated gestures: "We take the eye-ball *out*," (pretending to pluck eye from socket) "fix it, and put it back *in* again," (stuffing eye back in place). From then on I adored my uncle.

The night Shanku arrived we all slept in my father's old bedroom, my father and I in the large main bed and Shanku on a single a few feet away from it. It was a cavernous space, and during the day the far corners of the room were perpetually darkened by shadow, as if the night had once forgotten to adequately make its exit as the sun rose, and had been snared forever in the peripheries of the room. On a wooden table by the far wall stood two photographs, one of Ma and one of Burruda, whose life had finally ended in that same bedroom. Both photographs had been decorated in remembrance; a sandalwood 'tilak' painted over the

34

foreheads of both images and a garland of orange-yellow marigolds placed around each frame. As I climbed into bed that night, lifting the translucent mosquito-net that hung like a giant veil over the white sheets, I looked over at where the photographs stood but could see only the depthless black that had filled the edges of the room, waiting for the lamps to be switched off, and its chance to reclaim the house once more. I lay there in the stillness, drifting in and out of sleep until my father and Shanku came into the room, happy and tired after the large meal we had eaten that evening. My father climbed in next to me, scanned the interior of the net for any stray bugs, and switched the lights off.

He was awoken some hours later by violent movement. Slowly, so as not to wake me, he sat up. The entire bed was shaking, as if rapidly rocked by a hundred invisible hands. Frozen with confusion my father looked over at Shanku's bed, which stood perfectly still. His cousin had also been roused by the noise of our shuddering bed, and in the dark my father could see the whites of Shanku's eyes and the shocked gape of his mouth. Completely awake now, he gently pulled his sleeping son close to him and steadied himself by bracing one arm against the mattress. The shaking sent sharp ripples veering across the gauzy fabric of the mosquito-net, the sheen of waves on a restless black ocean. In the distance both my father and Shanku could hear cats screeching and wailing in the garden below. After thirty seconds or so the shaking stopped. My father and my uncle stared at each other in silence as the still night closed back around us like a hand.

When I awoke in sunlight to the sounds of Baba's regular morning sinus-clearings – a particularly Indian habit of hacking up phlegm and spitting it loudly off the

35

balcony into the garden – I was surprised to find myself alone. When my father appeared as I was eating a breakfast of sandesh (a sweet which I consumed in great quantities) he seemed tired but otherwise composed. I learnt much later that he had spent the whole morning quizzing the other family members and the house-servants as to whether they had felt any earth-tremors or vibrations during the night. No one had. Shanku had gone into town and asked whoever he met whether any large delivery lorries, perhaps on their way to Calcutta, had rumbled through the town that night. Nobody seemed to know.

When I wandered out into the garden that afternoon I found a group of ten or eleven cats sitting in the oblongs of sunlight which were draped over the grass, or perched on the stone garden walls. As I approached several of them began sniffing around my legs and circling me with curious, hesitant movements. They were thin, untamed animals and their eyes seemed to hold within them an unfamiliar intensity, not present in those of our pet cat at home in London. As they nudged their hard compact heads against my shins I looked up at the house. It was one of the last times I would regard the house like this whilst it still belonged to my family. By the time four years had elapsed Baba, Jethi and Jetha would all have died, and the house-servants dispersed into the dust of Bankura town. The house itself would remain empty and unkempt for a time, while the new owners, themselves close family friends, decided how best to use its grand spaces and imposing geometries. My father would not tell me of the incident in his old bedroom until many years after our visit. For some of the time he kept the story secret he did so for fear of frightening me, but as time went on he remained silent for deeper and more private reasons that could only be overcome, it seems, when his son had become a man.

But for now his son is an eleven year-old boy, gazing up at his father's family home as sunlight filters through the canopy of a mango tree, casting an alphabet of shadows over the crumbling burgundy walls. For this child there is nothing but the beat of life in the forms he sees around him, and in the faces of the aged relatives who have so warmly taken him in, folding themselves around him like a blanket.

To him, this dream of life is one he is only just beginning to understand.

JAY BASU

Heart's Desire

"Not a drop so far," Eamonn said. "Maybe we'll have a dry day of it after all."

Mary leaned her head against the window and closed her eyes. Over the radio, someone was announcing the names of the local children who had made their First Holy Communion that week. She smiled. You'd never hear that in Dublin, she thought. But this was the West, Yeats Country, "Land of Heart's Desire", as her husband liked to call it. He'd brought up the trip over breakfast a few weeks ago. A day in Connemara, another in Yeats Country, and a night at the Great Southern Hotel in Galway. She poured his tea, yawned, and nodded. She hadn't been to Galway in years, and the details of the place were starting to fade. It was just as well, she thought. The memories of their youth together were becoming harder to sustain with each year that passed, each year as they grew older and settled into silence.

Eamonn had first brought her here forty-five years ago, when he was finishing up his dissertation on Yeats. Mary hadn't read much of him then, just a few poems she'd been forced to learn in secondary school. She preferred novels, especially if they were set in distant places, like Zanzibar or Formosa. But Eamonn had always scoffed at her books, which wasn't fair, she thought. She never scoffed at his.

They'd come back to Sligo every few years since that first trip, when Eamonn had proposed to her on the banks of Glencar Lake. He was just a student then, restless and intelligent, with none of the pint-clutching, standoffish manner of the men she gone with before. No, Eamonn was all fast talk and fast movements, ready to pounce on another's words if he found them dull or ignorant. She

39

remembered the night they first met, at a UCD dance, how he had pulled her out onto the crowded dance floor without so much as a *May I* and how she had not protested, just danced, just stared at the crimson handkerchief in his coat pocket. It was the handkerchief, so red and flashy, that had got her attention that night. *It's strange*, she thought as she stared out of the window, *the things that first lead you to people*.

And then, awaking out of her reverie, she heard her husband's voice.

"Mary, will you look there!"

Mary opened her eyes and saw a girl in the distance. She stood with one hand on her hip, the other extended out over the road, thumb upright, a broad, easy-selling smile on her face and a backpack at her feet.

"I suppose we ought to pick the poor thing up before some luny grabs her," Eamonn said.

They pulled over without further discussion as the girl bolted toward the car.

"We're going to Sligo if it's any use to you."

"Great!" the girl said breathlessly.

She settled into the back seat as they pulled back out onto the road. Mary watched her through the rear view mirror, staring attentively out the window. She was thin, tan, blue-eyed and blond. The lads must be lining up for this one, Mary thought as she took her eyes away.

"So," Eamonn began, "you're from the States, are you?"

"That's right."

"What part?"

"Boston," she said eagerly.

"Boston… loads of Irish there I should say."

"Oh yeah, tons."

"And have you relations here in Ireland?"

"Yeah, somewhere down in Cork, but I don't really

know them. Their last name's O'Sullivan."

He laughed. "Should be a bit difficult, I imagine, tracking them down."

"Yeah," the girl said, "I'm not even gonna bother."

"And are you on holidays?" Mary said. She looked at the girl through the rear view mirror.

"Well, not exactly. I took a year off from college to travel around Europe."

"So you're a bit of a nomad then," Eamonn said, eyes still on the road.

"Yeah, you could say that."

"And are you enjoying your stay here in Ireland?" Mary said, shifting in her seat to face the girl.

"Oh yeah, I love it! Really, it's my favourite part of Europe so far. The people are so nice!"

"You're not on your own are you?" Mary asked.

"I am actually. Just me and my backpack."

"Well," Mary said, surprised.

Eamonn scrutinized her through the rear-view mirror. "And have you no friends or fellas who you'd want to see the world with?"

"Sure, I've got friends at home, but they're still in school."

"I see."

"And you don't mind bein' on your own?" Mary asked.

"No," the girl said, smiling. "I love it, to tell you the truth. I can go wherever I want and I don't have to answer to anyone. I mean, it's lonely sometimes, but usually I meet interesting people who've been all over."

"What kind of people?"

"Mostly Australians, I guess. They're the real travelers… don't go home for years. I hope to go next summer, if I can get the money together. I've got so many addresses, you know, from people I met on the road."

"Did you hear that, Mary," Eamonn said. "It seems as if we've got ourselves quite an adventurer."

"I should say so."

"And what age are you?" he asked.

"Nineteen."

"Nineteen! Hitching around Ireland on your own! By God you're a brave girl."

She laughed shyly.

Imagine that, Mary thought. Nineteen and traveling on her own, with no one to protect her. Hitching was a fairly dodgy way to get around, even in Ireland, and she wondered if the girl was truly aware of the dangers. She thought of that poor American girl, Annie Sullivan – if that was her name – who'd just disappeared one night a year back on her way home from a pub. Wicklow, was it? Mary wanted to tell this girl the story, but the sight of her – nearly bouncing on the back seat with excitement and energy, her big eyes drawn to the passing landscape – made Mary hold her tongue.

"So what brings you to Sligo?" her husband asked.

"Same as everyone else, I guess."

"Ah ha!" He hit the steering wheel with his palm. "Are you speaking about the man himself, our old Wandering Aengus?"

"Yeah, I just love his stuff."

"Really." He brightened. "Anything in particular?"

"All of it I guess."

She started to talk about Benbulben, Glencar, Lissadell House; Maud Gonne and Lady Gregory; Synge, the Abbey Theatre, the Playboy riots. Mary could tell by her husband's unconscious nods and attentive silence that he was pleased and a little amazed.

"And where, may I ask, did you learn so much about Irish literature?" he asked.

42

"Well, it's kind of my thing... you know, what I study at school."

"And where would that be?"

The girl shifted in her seat. "Harvard University ... it's in Bos –"

"Oh I know where it is! I know very well!" He smiled at her in the mirror. "You must have brains as well as beauty, then."

Oh will you listen to him, Mary thought to herself.

"I'm a professor of Anglo-Irish literature myself, over at UCD," he said.

"You're kidding," the girl said, smiling. And then they started to talk again about those things that Mary had learned, over the years, not to listen to. She let their words wash over her, like a language she did not understand. For thirty years, she had been dragged to department Christmas parties, dinner receptions, and university outings. For thirty years she had had to endure *their* talk, their meaningless jargon which gave them so much meaning: *deconstructivism*, *formalism*, *postmodernism*. What was the newest one? Oh yes, *cultural materialism*. She had stood always at his back, listening not because his words were interesting or witty but because, simply, she had nothing to say. When they were young there had been camping trips to Lough Erne and nights at the theater, holidays on Inishbofin and the odd weekend in London. But now he spent all his time with his books and she felt with every year that passed she knew him less and less. Soon, she figured, she would not know him at all.

"Well I agree with you that Yeats was not quite the Republican he claimed to be," Eamonn said to the girl, "but I wouldn't go so far as to call him an outright Brit."

"Yes but don't you think that the Anglo-Irish revival was just another attempt by the Protestant Ascendancy to

43

regain hegemony over Ireland. What about 'To a House Shaken in Land Agitation'?"

He nodded.

"If you ask me," the girl said, "Joyce was the real nationalist."

Mary saw her husband's eyes widen, the same way they used to at the Galway races, when his horse took the lead.

"I'm of the same mind myself," he said. "Just finished a paper on the subject, actually."

"Really? And I thought I was the only dissenting voice!"

"Well that's what Joyce wanted – dissent, arguments, unresolved tension. All quite beautiful, really."

Mary wanted to laugh. She'd once picked up a copy of *Ulysses* lying open on Eamonn's desk and started to read. *Ineluctable modality of the visible: at least that if no more, thought through my eyes. Signatures of all things I am here to read, seaspawn and seawrack, the nearing tide, that rusty boot.* She shut the book quickly as if it contained pornographic material. And it may as well have, for she never looked at him quite the same way again.

They stopped for lunch at a pub just outside Sligo. Mary stayed silent as the two continued to talk. Slowly she became interested in the girl, who seemed more sure of herself as the conversation progressed, and more articulate. She also seemed to be very intelligent. Mary knew her husband didn't just argue with anyone.

"Mrs. Donnelly?" a voice interrupted as she sipped her soup.

"Pardon?"

The girl smiled at her. "What do *you* think of Yeats?"

"Yeats?"

"Do you like him?"

44

Mary didn't know what to say, which was ridiculous, like having lived in a foreign country for forty-five years and still not being able to speak the language.

"Why, yes, I do. I like him very much."

The girl smiled. "What's your favorite poem?"

"Oh you know … that one about the hazel wand …"

"'The Song of Wandering Aengus.'" The girl smiled at her again.

"Yes, that's the one."

"Oh come on now Mary," her husband said gently. "That's too easy."

"Easy?" Mary smiled at him, the way she would have smiled at one of his colleagues. "Eamonn you've spent a lifetime trying to convince me otherwise."

He looked at her and said nothing. It came so rarely for her: to speak, and not be spoken to.

"Well I think it's a great poem," the girl said. "It's too bad they had to mention it in *The Bridges of Madison County*. Commercialized it, you know?"

"*The Bridges of Madison County*," Mary repeated. "I've never heard of it."

"It's a bestseller in the States right now, a real tear-jerker."

"What is it about?"

"Lost love, basically."

"Well it must be very new if I haven't heard of it. I work in a library, you see."

"Really? So do I, during the school year."

"Mind you, I haven't got any of those fancy qualifications they require these days, but my husband was good enough to speak to some people in his department … after the children left of course."

"It's a great job, don't you think? Peace and quiet is so rare these days."

Mary had never thought about it that way. It was something she had always downplayed in conversation, her unglamorous job, surrounded by books and dust and spinsterly supervisors. But something about the way the girl spoke about it made her feel differently.

"Yes, I suppose you're right."

"Well," Eamonn interjected, "I suppose we'd best be getting on if we want to see Benbulben by twilight."

Eamonn paid the bill and the three of them strolled outside. The clouds had receded and above them now was only a sharp blue sky punctuated by a small gold ring of sun.

"Will you look at that," her husband said, face to the sky. "Not a cloud."

They reached the outskirts of Sligo by late afternoon. They were quiet in the car as they neared the roundabout.

"Now what would you like to do, Shannon," Eamonn said, "stay with us and do a bit of touring? Or would you like us to drop you off in town."

"If you don't mind, I'd just as well stay with you."

Mary was strangely relieved.

Their first stop was Drumcliffe churchyard. Eamonn and the girl headed for the grave while Mary waited in the small cafe nearby. She observed them standing before the headstone, reverent and silent, and again she wanted to laugh. Dead men, lost words. That was what her husband lived for now.

After a while Eamonn came back into the cafe. He sat down with Mary and they drank their tea together in silence. When they were finished they got up and headed for the car. They thought the girl would be waiting for them outside in the parking lot, but when they saw her, she was still standing over the grave.

They reached Glencar Lake late in the afternoon. As usual Mary was filled with a rush as it came into view, remembering the heart-tightening excitement of that day, over forty-five years ago now. She looked over at her husband but his face was blank.

When they reached the parking lot he stopped the car and the three of them shuffled out. They began to walk towards the shore but suddenly Eamonn stopped without a word and headed off in the other direction. The girl looked at Mary, puzzled.

"He likes to be alone when he comes here," she replied.

Together the two women walked along the edge of the lake. Occasionally the girl knelt down and ran her fingers along the water, creating small, delicate ripples. Mary walked slowly, relishing the feel of sunlight on her back. It was so unlike the kind of warmth she was used to, the raw warmth of stoves and turf fires. It was gentler, like bathwater.

"It's turned out to be a fine day now, hasn't it?"

"Beautiful."

They walked on silently for a time, towards the small bend at the end of the lake.

"You know, Shannon, I've been wanting to tell you, it's very brave how you're going about."

"It's not brave, just cheap."

"I don't mean hitching – quite dangerous if you ask me – I mean how you're going about, on your own. I'd have never done it when I was a girl. But times were different then, I suppose."

"It wasn't proper."

"No, not where I lived."

As they walked their feet crunched down upon the small

47

shoreside pebbles in unison, giving their stride a subtle rhythm that neither was quite conscious of.

"You know," Mary said, "this reminds me of a place I used to go with my girlfriends when I was young… a hillside in Bray. We'd take a picnic up there Sundays after Mass, and just sit and talk for hours about the most useless things." She laughed. "But we amused ourselves."

"What kinds of useless things?"

"Oh you know, young men and the like. Silly things."

"Why silly?"

"Oh, because all we did was giggle. No one could get a proper word out before the rest of us started giggling."

"It's the same with me and my girlfriends."

"Ah no, it can't be. You young girls have so much more freedom than we ever dreamt of. Freedom to talk about whatever you want, whether it's sex, politics, religion. It must be wonderful."

"Yeah, I s'pose I just take it for granted."

Mary smiled.

"I was planning on going to the States you know, before I met Eamonn. I was going to live in New York with one of my friends. She had a job in Macy's, if I remember. She just loved New York. She used to write me the most exciting letters."

"Does she still live there?"

"She moved to California last I heard, but we've lost track of each other, over the years. You know."

"You should have come over for your honeymoon."

"I'm afraid Scotland was all we could afford at the time. And then came the children of course."

"Well, maybe someday."

"I don't think so. Eamonn won't fly you see. He's scared silly of airplanes."

"Really?" The girl laughed. "He seems so logical."

"Well, he is and he isn't."

As they walked, Mary looked around to contemplate her surroundings. For the first time, it seemed, she noticed how calm the lake was. It had never been like this with Eamonn. He was always pointing to some spot or another, always reciting lines. Before she had been like a fish swimming just below the surface, observing everything through a murky haze. But now her vision seemed clearer as she watched the sparks of gold sun reflect off the water, as if she were seeing everything from above, now.

"So what made you leave the States?" Mary knew she was prying but she didn't care.

"I think I wanted to do something that wasn't already done for me."

"What do you mean?"

"Well, back home, it's like no one thinks anymore. Or maybe they just think too much. Everyone complains that things are getting more complicated, you know, with all this new technology, but they're not. They're just getting easier. You don't even have to get up to turn your TV set off anymore. All you have to do is clap your hands."

"My."

"Even love letters are going out of style."

"Now that can't be true."

"Well, that's what Derrida says."

"Who?"

"Jaques Derrida. He's a philosopher."

"Nevermind him, what do you think?"

"Me? I'm the wrong person to ask."

"Oh come on now. I'd imagine a girl such as yourself… well, I'd imagine they'd be linin' up for you."

The girl looked away, out towards the lake. She reached down slowly and tore a tuft of grass from the ground.

"Boys don't like smart girls," she said, and Mary knew

instantly that she had upset her, the same vague way she could tell whenever she made Eamonn jealous. There was the same manner of not responding that gave everything away.

"Sure that's not true at all," Mary said, flustered. "You've got my husband chattering away all afternoon, and believe me, Eamonn's no eejit."

The girl looked at her. "It's not the same."

Just then Eamonn appeared from the trees. He seemed to be walking toward them in slowmotion, Mary thought, his movements heavy and deliberate, as if he, now, were walking underwater.

"Will we get a move on, then? We don't want to miss our dinner reservation, Mary."

"No, no."

"Why don't you come on to Galway with us, Shannon. You could maybe eat with us and then we'll get you settled some place –"

"Actually, would you mind dropping me off at Lissadell House?"

"Not at all," Eamonn said. He looked at her for a moment, a little perplexed. "You're sure you'd not rather go on to Galway? There's loads more *craic* there than you'll find around these parts."

"I'll get there, just not today."

"It's no trouble …"

"Oh Eamonn," Mary said, "can't you see she wants to stay here for a while?"

"Yes, well, I just thought… well I suppose you have had a long day. Maybe Galway would be too much for you tonight."

The girl nodded.

"Well then," he clapped his hands and rubbed his palms together, "we should get going. Myself and Mrs. Donnelly have a long drive ahead of us."

They let the girl off at Lissadell House. Eamonn gave her their address and number in Dublin in case she was ever in town, or stuck in a bind. She said her goodbyes and thank yous and then slammed the door. She waved to them as they drove away. It all happened very quickly, Mary thought.

Eamonn sped back onto the N15 and drove towards Galway. Mary leaned her head against the glass of the window and stared out at the low hills, covered with dead brown grass, and thought about the things that would happen to her now. By nightfall, they would reach Galway. They would park the car across from O'Connor's, they would get out and walk along the promenade and he would put his arm around her waist and talk about the air, how there was nothing in the world like the air in Salthill to get the blood flowing. "A little color, that's all you need sure, a little color in your cheeks'll put the blood back into you."

They would eat dinner at the Great Southern. There would be chicken and wine for her, lamb and stout for him. He'd tell her about his newest idea while he cut his meat or buttered his potatoes, his face drawn down to the plate, his eyes focusing on the food as her eyes focused on him – the pink flush of his cheeks which she had always loved, the gentle angles of his face. She would listen to him and nod and say encouraging things, like a mother to a child, "Why, that sounds brilliant," or, "Very interesting…" Her phrases never changed from year to year, only the tone in which she delivered them.

After dinner, they would walk back to Salthill along the promenade, under the moonlight and the black sky that had always seemed to her to be the edge of loneliness. He would ask her if she wanted to go for a drink at O'Connor's and she would say no, it was a place for the young people now. In fact it had always been a place for young people, it's just that the two of them were no longer young. They would maybe linger on the strand for a minute or two and look at the moon, and then they would go inside. They would get ready for bed without speaking and then slide in next to each other. They would feel hot and cramped in the double bed because they were used to sleeping apart, now.

But there were nearly three hours between now and then, three hours in which Mary could sink into the irresponsibility of motion. She closed her eyes and thought about the girl, wondered how she was getting on. She realized abruptly that she would never see her again and became filled with a great, inexplicable sadness.

When he spoke to her, she pretended to be asleep.

HEATHER CLARK

The Gift of TV

After the show Lee was very quiet in the limousine taking us back to the hotel. He held onto my hand tightly, and kind of stared at it. I was looking out of the window because I'd never been in New York before and I wanted to see everything.

He hadn't either. He hadn't been in a limousine, too, though I had, with some of my clients back when I was working as an escort. They used to get limousines to take us from the restaurant to the club or from the club to the hotel they were staying at, sometimes they were their own limousines too, real classy ones with brand new leather upholstery and full-size liquor bottles in the minibars. The tv one wasn't even the biggest limousine I'd ever been in, either, and it was kind of old.

Lee'd got the bag the tv people had given us and he was holding it gripped between his knees. It was a Ronnie Fairchild Show bag – on the outside they'd printed the logo of the show, like the cardboard one in the studio, and a photo of Ronnie Fairchild. In the bag there was a videotape of our show, only we weren't supposed to let anyone watch it till it had been transmitted, a big signed photo of Ronnie Fairchild, a photo of us with Ronnie Fairchild and some stills of us sitting in the chairs in front of the cardboard logo when the show was being taped. There wasn't one of when Lee got down on his knees and proposed to me, though. At the time when he did it I wanted to giggle because I was thinking about how his *ass* must have looked *huge* on tv. (I was crying as well though.) There was also a Bible in the bag, and inside the front of it Ronnie Fairchild had written 'To Maryann Macarthur. May the blessings of Jesus Christ go with you in your new life. Remembering you in my

53

prayers. Ronnie Fairchild.' He'd spelled my name wrong. It's Mary-Anne McArthur. It was nice of him to give us the Bible though.

When we got to the hotel the first thing I had to do was to call my Mom and tell her I'd just got engaged. She was minding Amy for me as well and I was missing Amy real bad. You never know how much you can miss someone until you have a baby. It's not like being in love with someone, you miss your kid much more. You always want to know what they're doing and if they're ok and if they're missing you. So the first thing I said was "How's Amy?"

"Missing her Mommy."

I asked if I could speak to her.

"She's having her afternoon nap." It was around three thirty in Denver so I knew she should have been, but I thought maybe because I wasn't there she wouldn't be able to go to sleep. "How was the show?" my mother asked.

"Well…" All of a sudden I felt myself turning red and embarrassed, though I was smiling too. "Mom, I just got engaged."

"You just got engaged to *Lee*?"

"Yes." My voice went small. It's not that my mother doesn't *like* Lee.

"Mary-Anne," my mother said, "Mary-Anne, did you get engaged *on air*?"

"Sure."

"*On the Ronnie Fairchild Show?* Oh Mary-Anne," said my mother. I could hear that she was shaking her head. "Oh Mary-Anne."

I'd thought she'd be pleased. I was happy. Sure, I was scared too, but I was *happy*. Then my mom said, quite slowly and calmly, "Mary-Anne, are you sure about this? I mean, Lee Vincent, don't get me wrong, Mary-Anne, I like Lee, he's a nice boy and all, but *Lee Vincent*?"

"Lee's good." I said. "He's going to take care of me. He loves me, Mom."

"Well, he's not much to look at, Mary-Anne. And he's not got much in the way of a job, either. What is it, car mechanic?"

"He's a partner in the mechanics' firm," I said.

"But Mary-Anne, you were doing so well with that new job of yours. You were bringing home so much money. I always said you were smart. Sure, you fooled around in school, but now you're doing really well. You're too good for him, Mary-Anne. You could do better. And you're a pretty girl, too, with your hair and those big brown eyes."

Lee was sitting by me on the bed while I made the call. He had turned a bit away from me when my mom started saying all that stuff about him. I don't think he wanted me to see his face. Lee doesn't show his feelings much but he's very sensitive. At that moment he turned back to me and took hold of the phone.

"Mrs McArthur," he said. His voice was really loud and strong. He seemed old. He's only nineteen and sometimes people think he's even younger than me but at that moment he seemed like he was about thirty-five years old and in the military or something. "Mrs McArthur, I'm going to marry your daughter. I love Mary-Anne and I'm going to love her and take care of her for the rest of her life. I don't care what she's done in the past and I don't care what other people are going to say about her–"

This wasn't very smart of Lee because my Mom didn't know anything. She didn't even know what the show was going to be about that we were taping. But I was so happy at that moment. My eyes were crying but I was happy. I loved Lee so much and I knew it was the right thing to marry him.

I don't know what my mom was saying on the other end

but there was a *loooong* pause and then Lee said "Well, I guess she should tell you herself." He handed me the phone.

"*What was the name of the show, Mary-Anne?*" said my mother.

"The Ronnie Fairchild show." I said.

"Not the name of the *show*, the name of the *broadcast*! 'I stole my best friend's lover'. 'I used to be a woman.' 'I slept with my...' Oh, I don't know!" She sounded so mad. "You *said* something on air, Mary-Anne. You confessed something. *What was it?*"

It was only because Lee was there that I was brave enough to tell her. Before I went on the show it didn't seem like such a big deal. I knew *some* people wouldn't like it, sure, but I didn't think it mattered that much. But Ronnie Fairchild and everyone, they made it sound much worse. I was so scared to tell my Mom. But Lee was there and he had his arm round me and I knew as long as I had him to take care of me everything would be all right.

"*My boyfriend doesn't know I'm a call girl.*" I said.

What happened on the show was, it was about girls who worked as call girls telling people in their family or their friends, who didn't know what they were doing. I had to go on and I could see on the monitor that it said across the screen 'Mary-Anne. Boyfriend doesn't know she's a call girl.' They had Lee in a room where he couldn't see when I told the audience and Ronnie Fairchild about it. We came near the end of the show and there had been two other people before us, only I didn't watch them because I was still having my hair done and being made up. They did a good job, too.

Ronnie Fairchild was smaller in real life than he looks on tv, plus, I never knew men had to wear so much make-up to be on tv. Actually he is quite old, maybe above sixty, and he has a bald patch at the back of his head which you never see. I didn't think men with grey hair cared about bald patches. Also his glasses aren't real glasses, he just wears them on tv, because he put them on right before we started recording.

Lee knew I was going to tell him something but he didn't know what it was and he didn't know what the show was about, because it was me that had answered the ad at the end of a show and I had got him to come along with me for the trip to New York. I think he might have thought I was going to tell him I was pregnant again. He knew I'd been working as a phone sex operator, and he knew I'd been doing some work for an escort agency too. He was never too happy about the phone sex – sometimes I had a funny caller that I wanted to tell him about but he never wanted to hear. I always thought he kind of liked that I was an escort –- he knew how classy it was to go to all these places with the rich clients and I looked fantastic when I was all dressed up to go out. I had some nice clothes. Though once he told me he was scared I'd go and marry one of them. As if. They were nice guys mostly but they were old.

They brought him on and told him to sit down in a chair next to me and he took hold of my hand, and Ronnie Fairchild went "So, Lee, you're Mary-Anne's boyfriend, am I right?"

"Yes, sir." Lee said.

"And how long have you been together?"

"About fifteen months." Lee said. Actually it's more like *thirteen*, and even with that it's been on and off a lot because I used to get bored with him sometimes and break up, then get back together again when I thought I missed him.

"And you love her?"

"Yes sir," Lee said. He could never have a career in broadcasting, he answers everything so shortly.

"Well Lee," said Ronnie Fairchild, "Mary-Anne has something to tell you."

I don't know what I expected him to do when I told him. I thought maybe he'd be angry with me. Just for a moment I was even a little scared he'd hit me or something – I grew up in a violent family because my dad used to hit my mom sometimes and my mom told me this was because grandpa used to beat up my grandma when dad was a little boy, much worse, so he broke her ribs once. But anyway Lee couldn't have hurt me badly, not with all the audience and the tv people there, and Ronnie Fairchild. Lee doesn't show his emotions much so you don't always know what's going on in his head. I also thought maybe he'd break up with me. It would have been sad but I know I could have handled it. I've always had lots of offers. I look nice.

It was hard! It seemed like I sat there for ages. I was twisting a hunk of my hair round my finger – I didn't even realise I was doing it till I saw myself on the monitor! I just didn't know how to say it. I thought I'd better break it to him slowly so I went, "You know I've been working as a phone sex operator?"

He didn't say anything, he just nodded.

"You know I've been working for the escort agency and just lately I've had lots of money and I've been able to buy Amy lots of new outfits? Well I've been going with some of the men from the escort agency for seven hundred dollars." (I said the last bit real quick to get it over.)

Ronnie Fairchild said, "So, Lee, what do you think about the fact that your girlfriend has told you she's been working as a call girl?"

Lee sat very quiet for a bit and he held onto my hand for

the whole time, like I said. I could see the monitor and at one point the camera was on our hands, close up, him holding my fingers tightly almost so they hurt. Then he said in this really choked-up voice, like a client I once had that had throat cancer, "I'll love you no matter what you do. I'll always be here for you." Everyone clapped and the camera went round the audience and the monitor showed this old woman getting out her handkerchief and wiping away tears. I was crying too. It was an emotional moment. Then Lee started getting out of his chair and then he got down on the floor on his knees in front of me and asked me to marry him. When this happened everyone clapped *real* hard. Ronnie Fairchild said "Mary-Anne, are you going to accept his proposal?"

I looked around at the studio. Lee just looked so stupid down there on the floor but he loved me. He really loved me. He was looking up at me like big old dog or something, I wanted to pet him. So I just said "Yes" and they all clapped again.

After that Ronnie Fairchild let the studio audience say things. One lady asked me how it felt to sell my body for money and whether I liked doing it and I told her, "I don't like doing it. It's icky. But I like the money." A black woman with a big crucifix round her neck said "Honey, I hear you talking and what worries me is, you don't seem to have any guilt for what you do." They all clapped about that, so I felt kind of defensive and I told them "My little girl has thirty pairs of shoes now and before I didn't even have enough money to buy her disposable diapers." An old woman shouted out, "When I was raising my four children there weren't any disposable diapers," and they all laughed. Then this really poor-looking woman got up and said, "Let me tell you one thing. Your little girl would rather have a mommy with self-respect than all the diapers in the world."

Ronnie Fairchild said "That's right. Your daughter doesn't care how many outfits she has. She doesn't need thirty pairs of shoes. She wants a mother with enough self-respect to not sell her body to strangers."

Then one woman who looked about the same age as my mom stood up and said how lucky I was to have a man like Lee who wanted to take care of me in spite of everything. Ronnie Fairchild said "Do you have anything to say to that, Mary-Anne?" and I said "I know" and they all clapped again. Then a young black guy said "I think he's *too* good for her" and some people clapped. So I said "I know" again, sweetly, and they clapped some more, but then Lee got up and said in a real threatening voice, "This is the woman I'm going to marry and I'm not going to listen to anyone badmouthing her, so if you want to say that again then come over here and say it." Ronnie Fairchild made a face at the camera then said "Please – calm down" and everyone was whistling and clapping even louder. (The funny thing was the black guy was almost eight inches taller than Lee so if they had had a fight he could have messed Lee up quite badly, but no-one seemed to care about that.)

Then Ronnie Fairchild said "That's almost all we've got time for today. But first I have one more thing to ask Mary-Anne." His face had switched to a different expression. He'd been like a tv star before, just asking questions, but now he reminded me of the principal of my old grade school or a minister. He came and stood right up next to me.

"Today's show has been a lot of fun, but we're talking about something far more important. Lee, you've promised to marry Mary-Anne, to marry her and take care of her for the rest of her life. Are you going to do this?"

Lee stood up. He said, loudly, "Yes, sir" and sat down

again. The audience didn't clap this time; it was like it was all too serious. Then Ronnie Fairchild said "Mary-Anne, you've been given the chance to change your life, to live as an upright citizen, amidst all the blessings of marriage. Now you're going to give up going to bed with clients for five hundred dollars, aren't you?"

"Seven hundred." I said.

Lee stood up again. "She is."

"But Mary-Anne, are you going to give up *all* those immoral ways of earning a living? You're going to give up selling your body to clients for seven hundred dollars. But are you going to give up working for the escort agencies? Are you going to give up working the phone sex lines? And I want to hear it from you this time."

"I suppose so." I whispered.

Ronnie Fairchild put his hand on my shoulder. "The microphone's not picking you up. Can you say it again, louder?"

"Yes." I said.

I hugged Lee when the closing credits were coming down. His face hadn't changed. Ronnie Fairchild and the audience seemed to think a lot of him.

Sex with Lee was really great that night. He was slow and gentle. He's always slow and gentle but sometimes I get kind of irritated and I want him to hurry up or be more decisive, but this time I really loved it, every moment of it. It was because I loved him so much. Usually when we had sex I felt like he was just some kid but this time it seemed like he was someone really important, a saint or a hero or an important minister or something. The only thing was I'd put on this lingerie from Frederick's of Hollywood. It was so beautiful, red satin and lace with a matching garter belt, all handmade. Movie stars wear lingerie like that, and

Madonna gets things from Frederick's of Hollywood too. When I took it off Lee picked it up and looked at the label inside and said "Did one of your clients buy you this?"

I said "Uh huh," and instead of leaving it on the floor by the bed where it had fallen he took it and threw it across the hotel room. Then he said, looking straight into my eyes, "Mary-Anne, I'm going to work real hard and buy you everything you need."

Well, I knew he wasn't going to buy me Frederick's of Hollywood lingerie for a start. But it was sweet of him. "It's ok, I have enough lingerie already," I said. And he kept kissing me, all over my neck and my shoulders, and saying, "*I'm* going to look after you. *I'm* going to look after you."

The Saturday after the show was screened I was round at Lee's place when the doorbell rang. I went to open it and there was a man standing there. He was thin and tall and grey-haired, wearing a dark suit. At first I thought he was one of my old clients, but he wasn't; you could tell from the sort of suit he wore that he was a minister, and he had one of those little fish lapel pins. "Miss MacArthur?" he said.

I was surprised he was asking for me. It was Lee's apartment after all.

"Did you want Lee?" I was about to go and get him. He was in the bathroom fixing up a new shower attachment; I was going to move in pretty soon and he wanted to get everything ready.

"Well, I've come to see the both of you. May I?"

He stepped in, very polite, and I showed him into the living-room. Lee came out of the bathroom. That afternoon he was wearing short pants and an old t-shirt and he was covered with dust from the holes he'd been making in the wall.

"Hello, Lee," the minister said.

"Hello, Reverend Miller."

He turned to me. "I didn't think Lee would remember me! He used to come to Sunday School at my church when he was a little boy."

"That's right," Lee said. "Can we offer you something to drink, Reverend Miller?"

"Some juice would be fine, thank you." He was sitting on the edge of our old brown velvet couch, leaning forward with his elbows on his knees. I went to the kitchen to get the juice and came back with some gingerbread men I'd baked that morning with Amy.

He was very grateful, really polite. It was hot outside and I guess he must have needed that juice. He drank half the glass down quickly and then held it in his hand, almost in front of his face.

"Did you see us on the Ronnie Fairchild Show?" I asked.

"That's right, Miss McArthur. And that's really why I came. I think you guessed that, am I right?"

I said "Uh huh" and Lee nodded. I was sitting on the armchair and Lee was on the arm of it, perched with his arm round my shoulders. Protective again. I think he looked to the minister like he was suspicious about something, but he wasn't, I know that because I know him well, but the minister didn't and was looking a little nervous. I smiled at him to make him relax a bit. He smiled back, still nervously. "I can't tell you how happy that show made me."

Lee said gruffly, "Me too," and their eyes met. Lee doesn't make eye contact with people very often.

"Well, of course you would feel that way, Lee. For your own personal reasons, naturally. But what I had to say goes deeper than that." He was looking at me. And getting into his stride now, now he knew that Lee wasn't hostile. "As it

63

says in the Bible, there's more rejoicing in heaven when a sinner repents…"

Now I think I felt a little uncomfortable. But he gave me this really warm smile, looked around for somewhere to put his juice, balanced it on the arm of the couch and reached out and clasped my hand. "I can't tell you how happy I am that you decided to follow the path of righteousness."

"Thank you," I said. I felt warm inside. When people you don't know come and show their concern about you, it's a nice feeling. But at the same time it was a little strange, to know how much he would have disapproved of the work I used to do. I suppose it's not really strange when a minister tells you you're a sinner because, after all, we're all supposed to be sinners, but it is funny that he came round specially just to see us like this.

"I was deeply moved," he said. "But I came round really to offer the support and prayers of myself and all my congregation. It may not be easy –" he had very pale blue eyes – "but you must know that you're not alone. Lee, that was a very admirable thing you did yesterday. It was a courageous, loving, deeply Christian thing. And yet you don't attend church regularly now, am I right?"

Lee muttered something.

"And Mary-Anne, you have a little girl, isn't that right? We still run a Sunday School, you know."

"Thank you, Reverend Miller." Lee looked at me. "Mary-Anne, I think we should go to church. And the Sunday School for Amy."

The minister was looking at me questioningly. I smiled. "Sure," I said. "It would be nice."

When he had gone I said to Lee, "So we're going to church tomorrow, right?"

"I think we should."

"I need to go home and pick up something to wear," I

said. "And an outfit for Amy."

"Ok."

"And we're doing the right thing?" I was kind of anxious. "Lee, I don't know if I still believe in all that – in the Bible and all. But I mean, we have to give Amy the chance of going to Sunday School, don't we?"

Lee didn't say anything else, he just nodded.

The minister mentioned us in his address. He said that there were new people in the congregation, and all that stuff about blessed be the sinner that repents, and not to judge. And that they should make us feel welcome. Everyone was looking round at who we were and I was glad I'd gone home to get the blue and white dress for Amy and that I was wearing a hat. After the service people came up to us and shook Lee's hand and a lot of the ladies hugged me and kissed me on the cheek.

We got married in that same church. It was just a small wedding. I wanted to wear a white dress but Lee's grandmother didn't think I should and she made such a fuss that in the end we said ok, I'd wear pale peach. She'd seen the show. She's very traditional. Amy was bridesmaid. She wore a little yellow dress with roses in her hair – she looked like a princess. The Ronnie Fairchild Show sent a photographer. Ronnie Fairchild sent us a wedding gift too: it was a new tv.

We watched the tape of the show quite a few times. When people came over they often wanted to see it. Everyone said how romantic it was, and they'd look from the screen to Lee and me. We were always sitting together on the couch at first. I think I got bored of watching it before Lee did. After the bit when Lee proposed I sometimes said "Come on, let's fast forward this bit" but he always wanted to watch it, right to the end. Then I started to get up and leave after this bit; there was always something I could say I had to go do, like wash the dishes or do the laundry. There always is something you can do around a house.

It was about a year later that I'd caught the bus up town to go look round the shops. I was just standing looking in a window when I heard my name called. I looked up and it was Clyde. In a new car. I knew him two years and in that time he had three new cars, and now there was another one. They belong to him, too, they're not company cars, and they're usually something expensive. This one was a Porsche.

"Hey, Clyde." It was good to see him. Of all my clients he was one I liked most. He always used to want to talk about me, ask me about my family and my girlfriends and what I was doing, like he wanted to know what my life was actually like. I mean this is rare because for most of the clients you just have to be like some kind of ideal fantasy and listen to them. Usually you have to listen a lot.

"What are you doing these days? I asked for you at the agency for a date the other week but they said you weren't working for them any more. What's up?"

"I got married," I said.

"Congratulations. How did you find him?"

"It's Lee," I said. I was a little embarrassed about this because I remember I always used to tell Clyde Lee was a loser and I was always going to break up with him and get someone else. He was polite though – he didn't say anything.

"That's great, Mary-Anne. And Lee doesn't let you go out on dates any more, right?" Clyde always called them 'dates'.

I just gave him a big smile.

"Well, maybe you'll let me buy you lunch. No strings, no nothing – we can go someplace nice."

I hesitated.

"I understand, you have to get back," Clyde said quickly. He was being tactful, too.

"No, I'm free." I didn't have to pick Amy up till four.

He got out of the car and went round and opened the door for me.

It felt natural to eat lunch with Clyde. In fact it felt even more natural than it used to do when I was working for the agency, since it was just lunch and we weren't dressed up or anything so people would have just thought he was my dad. I suppose in some ways he was the kind of person I'd of liked to have had as a dad. He was always so sweet. (He was one of the clients I'd slept with though. That hadn't been so great, though we'd done it more than just one time so it must have worked for him.) He is around fifty years old and slightly overweight though he says he jogs, and he hasn't got much hair left. He also has something wrong with his skin in patches where it flakes off but he doesn't look so bad really. Plus, he's a genuinely sweet person. Most of the guys I had to go out with were real assholes.

It was a real classy restaurant we went to. The menu was French though I'd thought it looked Italian and you could have pasta. "Maybe I'd like the steak" I said. It was so long since I'd had a meal somewhere really nice, I felt like I wanted to eat a lot. "What's *au poivre*?"

"That's with pepper," Clyde told me. "You never used to eat hardly anything, Mary-Anne. What's happened to that diet?"

It was true, I used to have salads whenever I went out. Clyde used to tease me about it. Most of the men I was escorting never noticed what I ate, except sometimes when they were the sort of guy who liked to order for you themselves.

"I burn so much energy doing the chores I don't need to be on a diet," I told him. Actually I'd stopped watching my figure. I don't know why. Sometimes I felt like I was eating a lot because I was mad at someone, though I don't know who. I never got mad at Lee or Amy, not really.

Clyde was looking hard at me. "So how do you like keeping house?"

I laughed. "You don't do it for fun, Clyde. But it's all right," I added.

Clyde shook his head, pretending to be rueful. "If I'd known you wanted to get married I'd have asked you to marry me," he said. "You could have had help and everything. You wouldn't have had to lift a finger. Shoot, I'll bet Lee hasn't even bought you a dishwasher."

"Actually *he* does the dishes, mostly." I'd picked a breadstick out of the basket and was eating it in that kind of flirty way, taking little bites and chewing them slowly, looking at him from under my lashes. Just then the waiter came to take our orders. Clyde leaned back, laughing at me a bit in a kind of snorty way. When we'd ordered he asked me, seriously, why I'd married Lee. I realised he must not have seen the tv show, so I told him about it and everything. He laughed out aloud.

"It's not funny," I said.

Clyde shook his head "That's just exactly like you, Mary-Anne. You go on tv to tell this guy about your work, he proposes, you end up married to him. So you gave up your work just so you could be on tv! Never mind. Just let me know when you've left him and you're working again, ok?"

I was really mad. It was like none of it was serious, like

68

I just stopped working because Lee told me to. It was my own personal decision, to stop it all and live as an upright citizen. And I wasn't doing it for Lee anyway. I was doing it for Amy. I told Clyde all this, really seriously. And he went serious too, and shook his head. "Come on, Mary-Anne. You know you were better off before. You could buy yourself the things you wanted, and for Amy too. You were having fun. You enjoyed every minute of that time you spent with me."

Well, that was hardly true! I started to say "But it was degrading!" but I managed to stop myself at "It was de–". Like, how can you say to someone that going with them was degrading?! So I just said "It was difficult. You know, with Amy and all."

"Fed up with being a single mom, huh?" Clyde looked really depressed. He was looking down at his empty plate – he'd had a Caesar salad because of his heart. "I can see it must be hard for you. In lots of ways." He started to fumble in his jacket pocket.

"No, it's ok." I didn't want Clyde to be sad, not after I was so happy to see him and he bought me lunch and everything. "I'm happy, Clyde. Really."

"Come on, Mary-Anne, you know you were better off before." He took a roll of money out of his inside pocket and he pushed it at me, across the table.

"What – ?" It was often the way clients used to make suggestions, when I was with the agency. It was bad news to be seen exchanging money in a public place because then if there was a cop watching you could be pulled in for soliciting. But it was easy because if I wasn't interested I could act all surprised and say, "I'm sorry, I don't think you understand. I'm an escort, not a call girl."

Clyde said, "I'm not propositioning you, Mary-Anne. And this isn't for you. It's for that little girl of yours. You buy something for Amy, understand? It's just a present from an old friend."

"Thank you, Clyde." You could see he knew how my mind worked because I wouldn't have taken it if he hadn't said it was for Amy. I put the money in the pocket of my jacket and through the rest of the meal I kept putting my hand in there to feel it. I hadn't had a chance to see how much there was exactly, but there were ten dollar notes and it was a thick wad, you could flick through it like the pages of a book.

When I'd picked Amy up from my mother's house I stayed to eat dinner with her; she said Lee'd called and was going to be working late. He did that a lot. When I got home at eight o'clock he still wasn't there, but the sneakers he wears for work were standing by the door and there was an empty glass on the drainer, so he must have been in and gone out again. Lee doesn't go out much but just sometimes he does, with his friends from work. He doesn't actually drink a whole lot, but sometimes he goes to a bar with them and has maybe one beer. The phone was off the hook, too.

I checked in the bedroom but he wasn't in there, and he wasn't in the shower either. So after I'd put Amy to bed I sat down to watch tv. There was some good comedy and stuff on. And I picked up a catalogue of childrens' clothes and began to go through it, picking out stuff I'd like to get for Amy. I often go through the catalogues but usually I couldn't afford anything in there. I'd counted the money Clyde had given me and it was more than two hundred dollars. It was so sweet of him. I think he has a lot of money but he isn't married or anything so he doesn't know what to spend it on.

There was a darling little denim jacket I wanted to get

for Amy – I love things like that on kids. I found a pen and drew a circle round the catalogue number. Then there was a little pink dress with a false apron thing – she loves dresses – she'd have looked like Dorothy from the *Wizard of Oz*. I was underlining it to show Lee and see what he thought and then there he was, standing in the doorway. He looked terrible. His hair was a mess and he had on his jeans he wears to work, with the oil over them and all, and a nice shirt, only there was something spilt down the front of it. At first I almost thought he was drunk, only Lee never gets drunk. He stood there in the doorway. I jumped up and ran over to him. "Are you ok, Lee, what's happening? Come on *in*." But he still didn't move, just stood there in the doorway. His hand were on the doorframe and he was leaning, swaying slightly. When I tried to put my hands on his shoulders he shrugged them back, like he didn't want me to touch him. "What's going on, Mary-Anne?" he asked.

"I ran into an old client. He bought me lunch. That's all, Lee. It was just like seeing someone from work, it wasn't anything wrong –"

"And the money?" I went to the mantlepiece where I'd put the money, and gave it to him.

Lee stared at the wad of money, he didn't make any attempt to see how much it was or anything. "He gave you this?"

"Sure." My voice came out small, like I'd done something wrong. "He said I should buy something for Amy. He has enough money, it wasn't anything to him. I can get her something nice, Lee."

Then Lee came right into the room. He grabbed something off the mantlepiece – it wasn't even anything of mine, it was a china clock in the shape of a racing car that belonged to him – and flung it into the fireplace, as hard as he could. Then he turned round to face me, and he said, not at all mad, "I'm not angry with you, Mary-Anne. I know you can't help what you did. Hell, you didn't do anything wrong. It's me, I'm just not enough – I'm just not doing well enough to be your husband."

"But –" I started to say, but then Amy started to cry in the bedroom.

Lee said brusquely, "Go and see to her."

When I'd made Amy believe that everything was ok and got her off to sleep again I sat and watched her for a while, in case she woke up again. And when I came back into the lounge Lee was in there watching that video, and when he got to the bit where he promised to look after me he rewound it and watched it again, and then when it finished he did it again, and again, and again.

The funny thing was, I didn't think to ask him how he knew about Clyde and the money, and it was only halfway through the next day when I came back from taking Amy to the clinic that I saw the light was flashing on the answerphone. Lee must have listened to the message when he got home the night before, because it said:

"Hello, this is a message for Mr Lee Vincent. You don't know me but I saw you on the Ronnie Fairchild Show lately and I think this is something you ought to know. I saw your fiancee today at 1.52 pm in the San Rafaello restaurant uptown. She was with a white man, about fifty to fifty-five years old, and I saw him give her money. They were sitting in the window of the restaurant when I went past and I saw it quite clearly. Well, I don't know what she's up to. You'll probably say it's none of my business. But after what happened on the tv and all, my conscience wouldn't let me rest."

It was a woman's voice; I don't know how old she was. Then the recorded electronic voice on the phone went:

'This message was received at 16.22 hours on Tuesday the –' I hung up and went to sit down, I actually felt dizzy. All the night before, when Lee said all that stuff, and when he wouldn't come to bed but sat watching the tape over and over, I never once cried or even felt like crying, I just felt like, kind of 'Well, ok.' This time I couldn't stop myself. I sat down on the couch and curled up with my head on my knees and sobbed. I was like that for about twenty minutes, I think. Then I got up, took the stupid videotape out of the machine, and wiped it. I recorded something over the top, I don't know what, just anything.

I was fixing supper that evening when Lee came home. He came right into the kitchen and stood there watching me for a bit. I was almost happy again by that time and I was humming to myself. I'm a happy kind of person, really.

"I've been thinking," he said.

"Mm-huh?"

"I'm going to call Ronnie Fairchild."

"What – ?"

"He'll know what to do," Lee said.

I shook my head and laughed. "But Lee, Ronnie Fairchild's a tv presenter, not –"

"*I want this marriage to work out,*" Lee said, really emphatically.

"Sure, Lee, so do I, but…" Then I stopped. "Go ahead. Whatever. I want it to work too, Lee, I really do."

Ronnie Fairchild wrote us a personal letter. It quoted some Bible verses and crap like that. He wrote that he was praying for us every night, and wished us success and happiness along the narrow but straight road we had chosen to follow. And that he had given our number to a friend of his who was a minister and experienced in advising young couples about their marital problems. So that minister came round and talked to us, too. Lee and I sat together on the

73

couch and the minister talked to us; Lee listened to every word and I tried to listen but I found my mind wandering off. I felt bad about this because I know I should have been trying more, when Lee was working so hard at our marriage, but I never was much good at concentrating. He told me I shouldn't have had lunch with Clyde because I should be avoiding not just sin itself but also temptation, which I suppose is true.

I told him about the phone call and how it had upset me. Lee had his arm round me and was stroking my shoulder when I talked about that, it was sweet of him. And the minister said that that was community, and that it was a wonderful thing that through the gift of television we could be brought together like this, that there were thousands, tens of thousands of people out there, who had been moved by what happened on the Ronnie Fairchild Show and as a result cared about my happiness and my spiritual welfare. And then he said, "Oh, before I forget." And he reached into his bag and took out a videotape and handed it to me. "Ronnie sent this, with his compliments. He told me your copy got wiped. Children *do* do that sort of thing, don't they?"

Lee took it out of my hand and laid it on the arm of the couch, as far as possible away from me. And then the minister went back to telling us how I should look up to Lee and follow him as a kind of moral guardian, and that in any case wives were supposed to obey their husbands, it was the natural thing. I don't know. It's in the Bible and everything, but I don't always know whether I should be following it. Magazines don't exactly say the same thing, do they?

Lee still watches the videotape of the show from time to time. It wouldn't be exaggerating to say it gives him strength. I never watch it though – it makes me feel a little sick.

Lee and I are still married and Amy has started school now. I work a few hours a week as a receptionist, though I don't make much money like that. It's harder not having money now Amy's at school because she has so many friends and she sees the nice things they have and asks if she can have them too and I have to tell her no, we can't afford it.

I love Lee and everything. He's good to me. I truly believe he is a good husband and everything. But sometimes I feel a little trapped.

KATHARINE EDGAR

The Descent of Dr Campbell

Pick a theologian, any theologian.

If, at 3.05pm on Wednesday the 8th of October, 1997, you had asked your chosen scholar to name the world's greatest living expert on comparative religion, he or she would not have hesitated.

"Anthony Campbell!" the unanimous acclamation would have rung out. "MA, D.Phil., Fellow of Magdalen College, Oxford. Author of such learned tomes as *The Twain Shall Meet: Links Between Eastern and Western Beliefs*, *Apollo Conquers Dionysius: The Religious Legacy of Ancient Greece* and *Some Comments on the Ritual Archetypes of Native American Tribes*. That's the man!"

Nevertheless, your informant would have been mistaken.

Since 3.02pm that same afternoon, Dr Campbell had been the world's greatest *dead* expert on comparative religion.

He had just performed an elegant swallow-dive from the top of Magdalen Tower.

At three o'clock, Campbell stood poised on the carved parapet, swaying gently in the breeze. He heard the hour strike beneath him, and gazed for the last time on the world he was leaving behind. Out of habit, he had carefully wrapped his glasses in a handkerchief and placed them in his pocket before ascending, so that all he could see was a blur of russet and gold, green and grey. It reminded him vaguely of a piece of Modern Art he had seen on his last visit to the Tate. He couldn't remember the name of the painter.

Not without grace, he launched himself into the soft air

and fell.

The sixty-year-old don was not in a state of spiritual despair. He was certainly not high, except in the literal sense. He had not even had his head turned by an excess of religion and decided that the prophecy *He shall give his angels charge concerning thee: and in their hands they shall bear thee up, lest at any time thou dash thy foot against a stone* applied to him personally. If we must seek out some deep psychological explanation for his suicide – and he himself would not have acknowledged that any such existed – it would perhaps be most accurate to say that he was a thwarted scientist.

Dr Campbell knew what the various Christian sects thought happened after death. He was intimately acquainted with the Muslim Paradise. He understood the principles and practice of reincarnation, even unto the precise gradations of birds and beasts. The Elysian Fields could hold no mysteries for him, nor Hades, nor the various realms of ancestor spirits. He was also well aware how many people believed in total extinction, and why.

He knew more than any other of those who study the beliefs of their fellow men, and enough for all of them put together. But, for A.A. Campbell, it was *not* enough. With a fiercely burning academic passion, he wanted to answer the final question. He had neatly framed the various hypotheses which the human race had come up with over so many millennia. Now it only remained to test them. With scientific scrupulousness, he believed none, considered – or tried to consider – all.

He might be snuffed out like a candle flame. He might be reborn. (He had calculated that he was probably worthy of a small chimpanzee or marmoset.) He might be forced to inhabit any one of hundreds of ghostly half-existences or uncomfortable Hells. Browning's

> *Twenty-nine distinct damnations,*
> *One sure if another fails*

were as nothing when compared to *his* prospects. For that, of course, was the one certainty. Salvation was not an option. To believe fervently in any one particular hypothesis might prejudice the experiment. He was in a state of perfect agnosticism, worthy of the scientist he might have been.

Or almost perfect.

There was once a very obscure tribe of American Indians with an anthropologically fascinating theory about the afterlife. They believed that only a few fortunates would be saved. The elect were to be that happy band of men and women who had been marked out as divine by their possession of the ability to waggle their ears.

It was their great tragedy that, over the last few centuries, no recorded member of the tribe had ever inherited or acquired such an enviable skill. Dr Campbell's account of their desperate attempts at ear exercise, as old age hastened on, and death drew near, was one of the most moving and admired passages of his *Comments*.

By a strange coincidence, Campbell's own ears were agile in this special way. Thus, his conviction that salvation was not for him shows that one religion, at least, he had rejected outright. We should not lay too much emphasis upon this single flaw in an otherwise blameless researcher. It was, after all, a remarkably silly idea.

It would be tasteless to dwell upon this great man's inevitable and untidy conjunction with the pavement.

The soul of Anthony Ambrose Campbell opened its

eyes, noting automatically that it appeared to have retained them. Noticing its noting, it noted that it still had its notebook and trusty old yellow fieldwork pencil. A spot of introspection informed it that, so far as it could tell, its identity appeared to be in place as well. These fundamentals having been established, Dr Campbell unwrapped his spectacles, polished them up, hooked them on, and looked about him with stern interest.

He was standing amid tall, golden grass. It rippled as breezes ran through it, stretching – he turned around and checked carefully – as far as the eye could see in all directions. This was not, admittedly, very far, as the grass was about six feet high, and Campbell had not been an imposing man. The sky was deep blue and cloudless; the sun, although bright, was not excessively hot.

The professor sat down cross-legged and recorded all these details. Then he thought about them. It was something of a blow not to have been transported directly to whoever was in charge, but it seemed to be received wisdom that some authoritative figure would turn up eventually. Had he been reincarnated, it was hardly likely that he would have retained his old brown suit. Unless something nasty was waiting around the corner, this was none of the seventy-two hells he had catalogued so exhaustively.

Dr Campbell allowed himself a small, satisfied smile. Insofar as he had been unable to avoid a preference, it had certainly been for some kind of neutral territory. Eternal torture sounded painfully monotonous. Indeed, when he considered what might have been, he felt rather sprightly. He parted the grasses ahead of him with enthusiasm, and trotted away to find out what was happening.

For a long time, nothing appeared to be happening. For a *subjectively* long time, he corrected himself. It was a little early to be drawing conclusions about the temporal aspects of eternity, so long the subject of such fierce academic controversy. (He had contributed his own mite to the debate in his day.) The sun was motionless. He was not hungry or tired, and had a suspicion that he could never be either again. Then he heard a voice. It was a deep, rolling, masculine voice.

"*Hearts*," it said, in tones no man would dare contradict.

The sound had come from straight ahead, and Campbell pressed on, seized by scholarly excitement. Was he about to meet God?

If so, God had an Australian accent.

"Are you a blind dog?" it demanded.

Campbell, wondering vaguely whether it was Judgement Day, and what he was supposed to reply, scribbled the words down in his notebook and hurried even faster. He thrust aside a final handful of grass and found himself in a small clearing. Three men and one woman, who had been sitting on the ground in a tight circle, turned around to stare at him. He stopped, panting and trying to catch his breath.

The woman rose. She was wearing a long purple tunic, Grecian in style, and her rather brassy golden hair was piled atop her head. (Surely *not* the Elysian Fields, he thought.) Her face and figure were middle-aged, but attractive.

"Do you play whist?" she enquired.

A man who has been a university lecturer for thirty years is used to answering difficult questions on his feet. But, on this occasion, Campbell was quite unable to speak. He goggled. The three men were also standing now, and he could see a number of ancient playing cards scattered on the ground behind them. The youngest spoke, but not to him. He had long blond hair, sulky eyes, an elegant short tunic and reminded the don of a particularly recalcitrant student.

"For the gods' sakes, Helen!" he snapped. "No more whist!"

She gave him a cold glance, and the greying man in bronze armour scowled. "You talk too much, Paris. You always did. Can *you* think of anything else to do?"

The lad looked mutinous, and the fourth member of the party stepped forward quickly. He was a mild, elderly man wearing a sparse tonsure, a baggy black habit, and over-large sandals. His was the voice which bore such a remarkable resemblance to that of God. Except, of course, Campbell hoped, for the Australian accent.

"Now Paris, Menelaus," he said soothingly, patting each of them on the head, "let's remember what we agreed about forgiving each other's trespasses."

There was a fraught pause, and the distracted professor suddenly found his voice. "Excuse me, madam," he addressed the lady, with a dated little bow, "but are you, by any chance, Helen of Troy?"

This turned out to be an unfortunate *faux pas*. The warrior rounded upon him viciously. "Sparta!" he hissed.

"Troy," muttered the young man, although without much conviction.

The woman looked supremely uninterested, and the monk sighed. "Why don't we say, Helen of the Aegean?" he suggested patiently. "Or would it be the Adriatic? I always mix them up."

Campbell was spluttering by now. "Then we *are* in the Elysian Fields?" he demanded.

"Oh no," said the monk, "I don't think so." He beckoned the don over to the far side of the clearing, while the other three sat down again. Menelaus shuffled the deck. "I'm afraid poor Paris wouldn't really qualify for Elysium," he whispered. "He's not exactly a hero, you see. Nor am I, of course."

"But this *is* the afterlife?" Campbell tried.

The monk looked perplexed. "Well, we're certainly all dead," he admitted. "But I wouldn't like to think that this was all there is. The Scripture clearly states –"

The professor's researcher's soul took over. He waved his pencil authoritatively. "May I have your name, please?"

"Brother Francis," said the monk.

"Now, Brother Francis, I want you to tell me, in your own words, precisely who you are, how you got here, and what you have experienced since your arrival."

A medium-size chunk of subjective time later, Dr Campbell sat down and flicked through his notebook. He had discovered the following facts:

1) There were a number of individuals and groups settled here and there in the grass, whiling away the time as best they could.

2) The monk could think of no common factor linking them.

3) The plain appeared to go on forever.

4) The environment remained constant, including position of sun, colour of grass, etc.

5) A resident arrived with everything he had been wearing at the moment of his death. (Paris claimed not to be able to remember where he had left his armour. Brother Francis had suffered a heart attack from the shock of finding a deck of playing cards in a fellow monk's cell in his small but strict religious community in Canberra in 1907, and inadvertently brought them with him.)

Campbell had known so much about so many things for so long that he found it oddly refreshing to rediscover the sensation of complete ignorance. He had no idea what to conclude from all of this. There were some interestingly primitive features…

A shadow covered his notes, and he looked up. The monk was standing over him, looking diffident.

"Well, well, what is it?" he asked, testily.

"I'm very sorry to disturb you," apologised Brother Francis, "but I wondered whether – that is, *we* wondered whether you knew – you see, I was seventeen when I found my vocation, and I never approved of gambling – that is –"

"*What* is?" demanded Campbell, not, he felt, unreasonably.

"Do you know any card games?"

It was when Helen won the fifty-third game of *vingt-et-un* that the doctor decided it was time to leave.

"After all," he pointed out to Brother Francis, with some severity, "I did *not* commit suicide in that spectacular but intensely painful manner, merely in order to sit around playing cards."

The monk apologised at once for inadvertently giving the impression that it had occurred to him to believe anything of the sort. "What *will* you do?" he enquired humbly, eager to make amends.

"Ahem," Dr Campbell began. "It seems to me that the first priority is to ascertain whether the locality is finite or infinite. Therefore, I intend to walk in a straight line towards the sun, questioning, as a second priority, any indigenous personnel I may encounter."

"How long will you do that for?" asked Brother Francis, in some awe.

"For as long as it takes," the professor returned grimly. His determined expression hinted that the afterlife had jolly well better co-operate if it knew what was good for it.

Paris, who had been lounging in the long grass, stood

up abruptly. "I'll come with you," he announced, eyeing the deck of cards with intense malevolence.

No-one could think of any reason why he should not, so he did. Brother Francis waved goodbye to them in an amiable fashion, and Helen inclined her head. Menelaus was playing patience, and pretended not to notice their departure.

The two men walked in silence for some time. Paris had never given the impression of being precisely conversational, and Campbell was writing down everything that had happened so far. When he had finished, he waited in vain for a remark from his companion. Finally, he searched his own repertoire of small talk.

"I've always been particularly interested in the darker manifestations of the cult of the Mother in Ancient Asia Minor – Ilium in particular," he tried, hopefully.

No response.

"How do *you* feel about the theory that the Trojan War was in fact an inevitable clash between earth-worship and sky-worship, with your abduction of Helen a subsequent invention by several poets calling themselves Homer?"

An expression of ineffable scorn crossed the young man's perfect face.

They walked on. Then Campbell had a thought. Anything was possible, he supposed. "Did you *really* meet Aphrodite?"

Paris spat. "The bitch got me killed, and for what?"

The world's foremost expert in comparative religion copied down his words reverently.

After that, the Trojan prince began to unbend enough to produce titbits of information concerning religion in Troy, Bronze Age life in general, and the internal politics of Olympus, about which he appeared to know an amazing amount. Campbell, who was already planning a sensational monograph (provisionally entitled *Homer Got It Right*), tried to reciprocate with a few little *bons mots* on the subject of various members of Magdalen Senior Common Room, but his companion didn't seem very interested.

They passed an Elizabethan gentlewoman and a Masai warrior at a distance, but neither came close enough to say hello, so they trudged on. Paris said that he had met the lady before, that her name was Katherine, and that she amused herself by weaving the grass into golden mats. He rather thought he had lent her his dagger with which to tidy up the edges.

"How kind of you," remarked the professor, feeling called upon to comment.

"That's what Brother Francis said," Paris responded, moodily. Then, suddenly, he stopped. He lifted his head and pricked up his ears, listening.

"They're coming," he said.

"What? Who?" squeaked Campbell, adjusting his glasses. He looked around nervously. Then he heard it: a low, heavy humming that seemed to fill the clear air. It came from somewhere over to the left, but it was getting louder by the moment. The sound became a drumming, then a thunder, and the ground began to shake. The don wondered whether he was finally going to get to meet some supernatural entities.

A herd of buffalo galloped past at full speed, flattening the prairie grass in a broad swathe. Silently, the two men watched the massive animals disappear into the distance.

Campbell was cast down. "Why buffalo?" he asked miserably.

Paris shrugged. "They just turn up occasionally." His ears moved again as he strained to hear the receding roll of the herd's retreat.

Moving ears.
Buffalo.
An endless prairie, for God's sake.

Campbell suddenly realised where he had to be. The plain shattered into pieces around him as he closed his eyes.

When he reopened them, he found himself in a drab, grey corridor. It stretched out endlessly in both directions and a cold wind blew through it. In front of him was a white door, adorned by a neat sign. It said, "Customer Services Department". Dr Campbell's hand twitched to take out his yellow pencil, but, angrily, he stilled it. Turning the brass handle, he walked through the door.

A man bearing a remarkable facial resemblance to the President of the United States was sitting at a small desk, writing. This threw the professor for a fleeting instant. Then he noticed something was missing.

"Where's Paris?" he asked.

The man looked up. He blinked, smiled rather apologetically, then began to leaf through a pile of papers. "I think it was the Elysian Fields," he muttered. "No, here we are. The Isles of the Blest." He put down his pen. "Same place, more or less," he added.

"But he wasn't a hero," said Campbell, blankly.

"I expect *he* thought he was. People often do, I believe. Why do you ask about him?" The man looked around vaguely, then he noticed a little yellow post-it stuck to his filing cabinet. "Ah, yes. Anthony Ambrose Campbell. You met a version of the poor chap in an Amerindian paradise, didn't you?"

Campbell sank down into a chair. "Is that all there is?" he asked pleadingly. "People who can wiggle their ears live forever, on a wide, golden prairie dreamed up by some shaman? No reason, no logic? No God?"

"Oh, there's certainly a God!" said the little man reprovingly, as if Campbell had suggested something in rather bad taste. "You can pop in to see him in a minute, if you like. And it's all most reasonable, I assure you. Every human being lives forever in perfect, eternal bliss." He beamed across the desk.

The professor frowned. "So why, may I ask, did I end up playing poker in North America?"

The Customer Services Manager sat forward eagerly. It was obvious that he had really been looking forward to this question. "You," he said, wagging a stern finger at Campbell, "were a very difficult case. Perfect bliss, you understand, is hardly perfect if one was anticipating something else entirely. The saints of Heaven would be quite upset to find themselves in Valhalla all of a sudden. And vice versa, of course. Most human beings have their own idea of Paradise. (A few people in the Middle Ages insisted on Purgatory, though I tried to keep it as brief as possible.) The atheists I put somewhere congenial on grounds of ignorance, last-minute repentance, that sort of thing. But one could hardly say that *you* were ignorant of religion, could one?" He chuckled.

"You knew about all the possibilities, and you knew that you were ineligible for most of them. The prairie was the best I could manage on such short notice. Plenty of room for research, which was what you really wanted, wasn't it?"

A peculiar thought struck Campbell. "Are you God?" he asked.

The little man blushed. And transformed into a figure at once awesome and inevitably *right*, as the office dissolved away into a starry sky.

"I am, as a matter of fact," He boomed, and His Voice

was the voice of an identical twin of Brother Francis, who had happened to train as a BBC newsreader. "Was there anything else you wanted to know?"

The don thought about it. Then he asked, a little proudly, "Am I the first person to – ahem – see through the facade?"

"Yes indeed. Nobody else has ever visualised the afterlife primarily as a research opportunity. You are the first client for whom we have had to set up this particular scenario."

Campbell registered this. And winced. "Are you saying that *all* of my discoveries were planned to suit me?"

"That's right, yes."

"Up to and including this conversation?"

"Of course."

There was a very long silence. Eventually, Dr Campbell sighed. "So what happens now?"

Golden infinity with a wise, white beard smiled at him. "What would you like?"

LAURA JAMES

Mrs Perkins' Anatomy

First Incision

I've always liked gloomy places. Some people are afraid of the dark, long for sunshine and summer, seek out the bright lights and the illuminated circle, but I like shadow, and shade, and murky corners. The purpose of the light is to make dark, and the purpose of dark to make light, but in between there lies a delicious shifting, slinking, wallowing of murkery where the shapes of unmade promises beckon. Turn the light on, and the promises resolve into chairs and empty bottles, demon and tempter has spots and the mysteries of savage Africa are actually your back-garden.

I'm not an optimist; quite the contrary. I think that it's best to be prepared for disappointment. I'm there when the lights go off and when the sun goes down. I know what it really is, but by allowing myself a small measure of realistic licence, I save myself a large measure of despair. In all other fields I am absolutely a realist, the little voice saying, no, you'll get into trouble, or, you look fat in that, and once, he doesn't love me anymore. But in matters of light and dark, shadow and shade, I occasionally let my imagination dip a toe in the water and paddle for a while.

It was this cautious freedom that introduced me to Mrs Perkins.

The dissection room is a place of green. I don't mean a verdant, enthusiastic, billiard table sort of green, but a weedy, swimmy, fishpondy sort of green, the sort of lurking-pike, dragonfly-skimming, evolutionary mud type green. The light filters down through thick plates of dimpled glass, detouring around the colonies of greedy moss before struggling through the panes and collapsing, gasping on the smeared pages of my dissection manual. It was there it lay when I opened page one, finding it panting its last on the instructions for nervous first years, telling me where to make the first incision, and it was there on the pages of my apprehensive colleagues. It also lay on the pale plastic sheet which swathed the undisclosed seventh member of our dissection team, showing a peak at the top end of the table, and a broader ridge at the bottom, while in between ran a gentle elongated mound, dropping away in volcanic folds to fall over the edge of the metal trolley.

We stood like an honour guard in our ill-fitting white coats, three on each side, shifty-eyed. I was on the right at the head, opposite Ben, a thin boy with yellow teeth and furtive good looks. To my right was blonde Sarah, then stooping Helen, who is not unattractive when she makes the effort. Opposite Helen stood Matt, who is attractive even when he doesn't make the effort. The last place, between Ben and Matt, was occupied by a little dark girl who had not yet introduced herself. Around the room stood similar arrangements of white clad strangers, a peculiar sort of heaven for the Bodies, if only they knew. The monitors around the room crackled into life, and the Lord of the Dead himself, Dr Lee, swam into view, his yellow skin flushed a frivolous shade of on-screen pink. He began his introductory patter:

"Welcome, Ia medics, to your first dissection session. You should all be wearing white coats and latex gloves that *fit;* if not, you can buy them from the technicians at the end of the practical. Most of you, I assume, are about to see your First Dead Body – hopefully, throughout your careers, you will not be seeing many more." The little dark girl gulped. A wave of dutiful amusement briefly swelled. "I know you're all eager to begin, so just a few words of advice before you get stuck in." The camera swung unsteadily to the demonstration cadaver. Dr Lee's gloved hands descended, toolkit in hand. He drew out the larger scalpel, and unwrapped a blade from a small flat packet resembling a stick of chewing gum. "When you put your blade into the handle, please be careful, and hold it with the tip *away* from the ball of your thumb." The sheet was drawn off the body, but the camera zoomed in to a patch of skin, so we couldn't see the face. "When you cut, feel the depth through the scalpel; we want to go in just laterally to the midline, come down to about the level of T7, just underneath the breast, or where the breast would be, then turn the corner and head for the side. When you've made that L-shape cut, you can lift up the corner of skin and pull it back to expose the thorax and axilla. You'll need to slide your blade underneath and stroke off the connective tissue, like this, to release it as you pull. Make sure your cuts are long enough for you to be able to fold back that piece of skin over the shoulder so you can see properly. After that, the demonstrators should be over to tell you what to do next, we'll be finding pectoralis major and minor, but just worry about the first incision for now."

I worried. I had seen a dead body before, but fully clothed and unpickled. The smell was nauseating, and I hadn't liked the way that clear, yellow fluid had oozed out from Dr Lee's incisions. Sarah nonchalantly started drawing down the sheet. At first I couldn't see what was underneath, then I realised there was a clear plastic body bag, tied at the head with striped cord, through which an obese yellow form showed, like an old, melted barley sugar in a wrapper. Sarah folded the sheet tidily over the waist of the body, then reached over to untie the cord. Ben got there first, apparently eager to begin his Medical Career, but I noticed his hand shaking.

"Who wants to make the cut?" asked Ben. We all started fumbling in our pockets for our dissection kits. Clumsily, I fitted a blade to the handle. No one volunteered.

"Don't mind," said Sarah non-comittally. "We'll have to get it out first." We all looked around uncertainly. The table nearest to us (we were in the far corner) were struggling to lift their cadaver by the head, getting in each other's way as they gripped and tugged at the bag. I took a deep breath and rolled up my metaphorical sleeves.

"If we –" I jerked my head at Ben "– can manage to lift up its shoulders, you two –" Matt and Sarah "– can roll down the bag." Gingerly I inserted my hands into the interior of the bag. It was wet and slippery. We slid our hands under the shoulders, and I gave in to the voluptuous sensation of dead, wet flesh. Sarah and Matt dragged down the bag. And as they did so, a sign occurred; a strong shaft of light bore through the pane-glass roof, coming to land on her face at the moment it was revealed, illuminating her features like a blessing. The intensity of the light ran over the clammy, yellowed skin, caressing the half open eyes and the bleached bristles on her chin, running over her heavy cheeks to drip and pool in the dank crevices of her ears: it paused on the heads of my partners in a paternal gesture, shining through their wisps of stray hair in fuzzy haloes. The Lord had spoken, as clearly as if he had used Dr Lee's microphone. The light had penetrated.

It took some arguing to decide on her name. It may seem strange to name a corpse, but given the intimacy of the circumstance 'she' would not do. Other people chose comedy names, Algernon, Tallulah, Engelbert, but we all felt that our Body was not comic. Some discussion was given to naming her after celebrities, but even Ben realised that sensitivity was required, a gesture of respect, an acknowledgement of our enlightenment. We discussed what she might have been called in life. Perhaps her mother was a romantic, had called her Penelope or Cassandra? Had she answered to Aggie for Agatha or Vi for Violet? Was she married? Did she live alone? Did she long for a sweetheart to save her from spinsterish penury, or did she revel in her solitude, broken only by the purring of cats? Where was she now, could she see Sarah methodically peeling away her skin, or Hannah recoil from the greasy blobs of adipose tissue spilling out onto the trolley?

In the following sessions, discussions would crop up as to the meaning of body and soul, and the relationship between them. Little Hannah emerged as a metaphysical, arguing that the soul was chained to the body, limited by corporeality, writhing and wrestling in its fetters. Helen favoured a purer dissociation, the soul a buried capsule inside the body which released its essence with death, the golden fragrance soaring above the domes and palazzos, like the sunlight in a Merchant Ivory film. Matt, Ben and Sarah preferred a more mundane series of conjecture – we soon passed beyond name and marital status to personal preferences and lifestyle – had she liked hats, or preferred hoods? In cold weather would she pace the towpath in sensible shoes, breath puffing out in little clouds of smoke, signals to tribes of expectant Red Indians? I enjoyed these conversations triggered by the clues we found on the treasure map of her body, but speculations on the nature of the soul, specifically, Her soul, did not interest me. I knew where She was and I appreciated Her fiercely. I was awed. Someone had given Herself wholly unto me, a noble gesture on an ultimate scale. I had seen the light come upon Her, and I knew that it was a message. She had spoken. I was chosen.

After that first session, I emerged from the green of the dissection room blinking in the diffused light of afternoon, and noticed how the crenellations on the college façade looked like the battlements of heaven, and I saw angels in the darkening streets.

Deeper Cut

I drew her as she had been, a blue study on an orange background, reclining nude on a cloud with a hand outstretched into her sunset. Tendrils of mouse brown hair became Mediterranean blue; blue shade carefully rounded out the heavy hips and stippled the bleached moustache. I blue-tacked her to my window so that the spires rose behind and around her, entitling it 'Mrs Perkins in the Ether'. The sun shone through the coloured crayon, so that I could see the veins marbling her legs, the pulsing arteries entwined around her viscera; I saw the breath in her lungs exhaled as though it were fizzing orange sherbet. I saw waves of contractions pass down her living gut, the busy war of the lymphocytes hurrying through her circulation, shouldering aside the burdened erythroblasts as they raced towards trauma sites and pathogens; I saw her live.

She began to enter my dreams. In the afternoons we worked our way through her rotator cuff, the subtle interconnections of her carpal bones, the convolutions of her rubbery arterial branches and the spaghetti junctions of her brachial plexus. During the night she worked her way into my head, sliding in through the external acoustic meatus, delicately tearing aside the tympanic membrane and stepping over the threshold of the middle ear, surprisingly graceful for one of her bulk. She rested in my epitympanic recess, running an absent-minded finger over the whorls and shelves of labyrinth as if looking for dust before taking a short cut into my nasopharynx by wriggling down my Euston Station tube. At the orifice, she paused and looked down at the soft, furry dampness of my sleeping pink tongue then launched herself into me, swimming up and up, passing through epithelium, bone and cartilage to enter the watery shadow of my limbic system. She curled up and hid, pulling my memories over her like blankets, silent in the rhythmic, internal twilight.

Her presence was unobtrusive. For long periods I could forget she was there while I struggled to stay awake in the lecture fug or slid my eyes along the line of visitors in the bar. I rode my bicycle to Jesus Green and played football undisturbed. She slept. I went shopping, and bought a dress for a Christmas party; it was dark red silk and made her stir a little, remembering an unsuitable party-dress her mother had once worn. She liked the market, opening a corner of an eye to check the chattering, and the cold feet stamping, and the heavy rotundity of a bought cabbage. From time to time she let me know that she was still there, knocking her blue fist on the vault of my skull so that it echoed and rang; the doves of my thoughts rose in a flock while the reverberations settled.

I began to see her. I didn't just see her on my window, or in a fleeting expression on my face in the mirror. I didn't see her as I had seen her in the dissection room, stripped of ungainly fat and skin, elegant muscle stretching into blue sheened tendon over a glimpse of refractive bone. I saw her in Sainsbury's behind the far checkout, pretending to be working but inspecting the goods with hungry interest. I saw her in physiology, high at the back of the theatre, taking notes with a scratchy fountain pen. I saw her through a car window as I waited to cross the road, I saw her in the early morning garden reading a book, I saw her in the chapel. I saw her, I saw her, I saw her, in every corner where the light fell slantwise, licking at the edges of window and book, but never falling on her.

I really did see her.

Viscera

Back in the seductive pond atmosphere of the dissection room, my colleagues had assumed the jaded air of seasoned dissectors. The moss on the roof was growing, avidly soaking up the gentle drizzle and enclosing it jealously in its velvet breast so that the fluorescent tube lamps had to be switched on earlier and earlier. Night began at about four o'clock; by six the only shadows to be found belonged to the light of inside, and the streetlights.

We unwrapped her now with little reverence – her head had disappeared overnight into the maws of the part Ib syllabus, and the headless, skinless, lifeless body was easier to lift out of the bag. She dripped and oozed, marinated in formaldehyde so that stray hairs or sleeves were likely to dampen, and shoes often had dark, wet patches. Gone was the open-mouthed innocence, the purity of leached yellow skin in illumination. The elegant form of bare muscle had been desecrated, muscles reflected and nerves carelessly torn; globules of fat and shreds of skin lay around her. The flexor compartment of her right forearm dangled tenuously off her median epicondyle. We were working on her abdomen now, and she lay in stiff-armed supplication, arms thrown out perpendicular to her headless trunk in wordless plea. The structures visible in the stump of her neck were ugly, bruised colours. Someone had wheeled hard clots of dark blood from the open carotid arteries and left them in a crumbled heap below.

The session in which we had to remove her intestines began badly. A student from the morning group had pointed out how the cadavers' last meals still rested in their digestive systems, undisturbed for the past two years during embalming, and we poked and prodded and squeezed in mock peristalsis, until Matt squeezed too roughly, and made a hole. The formaldehyde odours were at once swallowed up by something more brutal, and a bad mood settled. We had to tie off the duodenum, and cut it off at the top end, then do the same at the bottom to the descending colon so we could remove the guts and look at them properly. Ben read aloud from the manual as Sarah got on with the job. As I stood there, flicking the epiploic tags of fat on her colon in revulsion, and wondering about the state of my insides, she began to drum her heels on the back of my eye-balls, so that I blinked, then looked up.

She was sprawled on the roof with her face pressed flat into the glass. Where cheek and chin rested on the pane the skin had turned yellow, as it had been at first incision. Rain blurred her features, but I made out her fingers, remote from her face, scrabbling wildly away at the moss without strategy, her arms manipulating them in arcs on the pivot of her shoulder as though they were wings. Her hot breath misted the cool glass, the vapour condensing and mingling with the rain in the dimples of the surface. Her pale shadow fell onto the table, breaking Sarah's concentration. Sarah stood and straightened.

A green-coated demonstrator patrolling the tables felt the shadow, and switched on the lights. When I looked back up she had gone, and the rain was already obliterating the muddy smears of her hands.

Vapour

I felt uneasy. I had rather liked seeing her unexpectedly in town, behaving as she had. It made me feel protected, cushioned by the confirmation of my secret, the crystallisation of elusive liquid thought. The episode of the viscera; I had believed we had an understanding, an intimate agreement; my body for hers, hers for mine and the capsules of soul were our own. They would remain undisturbed, mine deep inside and hers released, but I didn't see her in the garden, reading, anymore.

It rained for the next two weeks until the end of term and the sky was thunderously overcast, emitting no light, generating no shadows.

I recognised the breaking of faith. I took her picture off my window, and concentrated on other things. She kept quiet.

One fading afternoon while I was half asleep she woke up, stretched and shook herself. She kicked down her blankets and smoothed her skirts, cocking her ear to hear the lapping of cerebrospinal fluid on the beach of my occipital bone. She clambered onto atlas and launched herself down the knobbly length of my spinal cord, using the ligaments to smooth her fall. She gathered up speed, sliding faster and faster and faster, until in a blur of orange and blue and red party-dress memories, she dissolved.

ANNA KHOO

Fortune's Goose

His name was Simon Fortune, and he was the biggest liar in the world. I met him at Christmas 1993, on the West Cumbrian coast in a small pub in a town called Egremont. Those in the know, he said, called it Excrement. He wasn't going to stay there long but he was, as he put it, between jobs at the time. In fact, he said he'd not been back long from Central Europe. A special mission to Hungary, to be exact.

I supped my pint and sat back.

It all started, he said, when he went to renew his RSPB membership. They said they were looking for someone to do a spot of research. They said that the incredibly rare collared goose had been sighted on the banks of the River Tisza in Hungary. He said that he was doing nothing that afternoon. So they sent him there in a roaring jumbo jet, all expenses paid. He said he obliged: all expenses spent. On arriving he took the bus to Lenintown and quickly settled in with an old Hungarian charlady who cooked his meals and socks in the same pan. He said that he then spent the next couple of weeks fruitlessly traipsing up and down the dirty, reedy banks of the Tisza, spotting nothing.

He admitted, however, that he'd never really been much good at bird-spotting. In fact, he said that back home he used to shoot them with an air rifle. It helped with identification. With the limp bird in one hand, he could turn the pages of his *Observer's Book of Birds* with the other at leisure. It was worth any number in a bush. His binocular hands were never very steady either, he said. They kept snagging on women getting undressed in upstairs rooms with the curtains open, only belatedly chasing rare egrets and eagles over the horizon. It was no different in Hungary,

101

he said. What was more, the natives weren't very friendly. They shied away, mumbling in Magyar, from this lanky blond Englishman with his binoculars always trained on their uncurtained flats. It was his charlady, he said, who eventually put him in touch with the locals. She encouraged him to join them in their favourite pastime of racing old bathtubs across the Tisza. He couldn't find a bathtub so he used a wheelie-bin. Although watertight, it wasn't quite as streamlined as their zinc tubs, some fitted with outboards. It didn't "cut the blue turf", as the locals said. In fact, they howled with laughter the first time he rolled his craft down the bank. Anyway, after a week or two of his coming last, he said that they dropped their reserve. Then a snaggle-toothed peasant with eyebrows on his cheeks told him about the collared geese. A pair of them had been spotted, the peasant said – spraying sunflower seed husks as he spoke – upstream near László Nagy's place.

Here Fortune stopped, picked up his pint then put it abruptly back down again. Did I know that in Hungary all names are back to front? Well they are. And he nodded in self-agreement. So this guy was really called Nagy László. Did I know what that meant in English? No? Big Leslie. Yep, this guy he went to see was called Big Leslie. So, he said, he went to Big Leslie's farm the next day. Early, about tennish. It wasn't so much a farm, he said, as a loosely timbered shack with a muddy yard in front of it where hens and pigs and dogs and ducks scratched around, eating each others' droppings. He introduced himself to Big Leslie who was busy feeding chopped eels to his mangy cat. He was a tiny bald man with kind eyes, he said, not big at all. After trying to imitate the harsh call of the collared goose, getting successively louder the more he was misunderstood, he said he had resorted at last to his *Observer's Book of Birds*, Hungarian edition, and pointed in it to the picture of his prey. Understanding and strange relief dawned on Big Leslie's face. By gesticulation mostly, he came to understand that a pair of white geese, with that distinctive shiny black-brown collar about their necks, had been sighted behind the farm, down where the Tisza lapped dirtily against the reeds. He had been invited into the farm, and took up a position in the kitchen overlooking the allotment and outside toilet which separated the house from the river.

He said that he waited a day and a night like this, fed kindly on eels too, till in the early morning light he saw two white birds waddling towards the house. He reached for his binoculars and *Observer's Book of Birds*, Hungarian edition, but the damn things kept waddling out of focus. So he whistled up Big Leslie, who appeared bleary-eyed and weary, and led him through to the back porch of the house. They were geese, he realized, but as they waddled closer he still couldn't be sure of that mark on their necks, so without thinking he asked Big Leslie for his air rifle. Big Leslie handed him a twelve-bore. With hindsight he shot the bird at perhaps too close a range. When the feathers settled, he said, he was lucky to pick up the beak and feet. Nonetheless among the sprayed giblets and feathers he found a strip of neck with that black-brown mark on it. Yet as he was turning over the pages of his *Observer's Book of Birds*, he noticed that the mark smeared on his fingers. Oh yes, said Big Leslie, laughing, the geese often came to the back door and stuck their necks through the catflap to get at the chopped eel. And Big Leslie then ran a finger along the edge of the freshly oiled catflap and held it up, black-brown and shiny, for inspection.

Fortune slurped his pint and shook his head. He said he'd never been so gobsmacked in all his life. So with nothing to keep him there, he said, he took the next flight back to England, and Egremont, and went immediately to the local RSPB office to tell them not to sent him on any more bloody, well – bloody wild goose chases.

*

Unbeknown to Fortune, I was working in Hungary at the time. In fact, two days after hearing his tall tale, my flight landed at Budapest's Ferihegy airport. From the city centre I took a bus back to Tiszaújváros in the east of the country where I was teaching English at the secondary school. Tiszaújváros was about my age, although it improbably had even less culture than I had. Of course, it had a Culture House, but that was one of the main reasons why it had no culture. It was a Soviet town, a new town, a socialist-realist town. It was made up of pigeon-grey concrete tower blocks arranged in squares and intersected by wide featureless streets. The grocers' and hairdressers' were built into the lower floors of the tower blocks, displaying lowkey purple and green signs. I imagined that at my first gesture of non-conformity the blocks of flats would uproot themselves and stampede me out onto the frozen unrelieved spaces of the great plain surrounding the town. Yet what spared me from certain alienation was the town's inhabitants, with their subversive humour, colourfulness and almost aggressive hospitality.

My first weekend there, I was whisked – if you can ever be whisked by Trabant – out onto the sear-yellow expanse of the plain and, in the mildness of a September evening, sat down to a thin spicy *gulyás* unlike anything I had ever tasted before. Back home, goulash was essentially shepherd's pie with the potato scraped off and a dash of paprika thrown in for exotic effect; here it was cooked in a black charred cauldron hung from a cleft stick over a smouldering open fire. The spices, the smells, the smoke were intoxicating. Later, too, shortly before Christmas, the husband of one of the English teachers took me to the powerstation swimming pool. This was an outdoor pool set directly beneath the towering, pluming chimneys blinking with red lights, and nestled in glittering intricate pipework. It was heated by harnessing the energy routinely wasted as it was relayed in so many miles of pipe. We changed in a small wooden hut then charged across a boardwalk of snow to jump into the steaming pool. And while we were there it snowed magically, swirling down past the blinking red lights of the gigantic chimneys, melting instantly on the silvery pipework. The steam rising from the pool and the snow falling met in a mysterious zone of suspended water, being neither crystal nor vapour, about a foot off the pool's surface, on the crest of my head. I just stared upwards, letting flakes melt in my upturned mouth.

In addition to these singular treats, I was also invited to play football every Tuesday night in a junior school gym, in the company of eight or nine overweight teachers, marvelling at their close control as the ball ricocheted off wallbars and crashmats, marvelling also at their hairy backs matted by an unstaunchable flow of sweat. They greased and glanced off each other as I panted about between them ineffectually, running to wherever the ball had just been. At half-time they tippled pálinka, the sort of short that evaporates through the roof of your mouth and sends you temporarily blind.

All in all, then, I got on famously with my fellow teachers and their spouses. Of course, this made me all the more reluctant to tell them Fortune's tall tale. Nonetheless, I was fascinated by the sheer ludicrousness of it and wanted to pit it against reality. So one day, after yet another enthusiastic forty-five minute session of "Hangman", I asked Timea, the youngest of the teachers, if she knew anyone called László Nagy. She laughed riotously: did I know anyone called John Smith? My question, it seemed, had all the precision of a three-line horoscope.

"Why?" she wanted to know.

"Oh," I said, stalling. "Nothing really."

I was ashamed ever to have brought up Fortune's woolly yarn. So I lied. I told her that on TV back home over Christmas there had been a series on foreign film stars in Hollywood. The series had reached the 1950s and it had mentioned one László Nagy who was apparently a great Hungarian matinée idol, all teeth and brylcreem, yet who had missed the plane to the States when the Uprising broke out in 1956, and so was left behind on the runway to wave off the likes of Tony Curtis and Zsa Zsa Gabor as they soared off to fame and fortune. Now, I said, he is supposed to be living somewhere round here.

"Never heard of him," she said. Then in a more conciliatory tone: "I'll ask my dad."

"You needn't."

But she did. And her dad said that he knew a László Nagy in near-by Tiszalök, although he doubted he was ever a film star.

"Perhaps I got the name wrong," I said lamely that weekend as Timea's Trabant trundled the pair of us over the bleak plain in search of László Nagy, the soi-disant '50s dreamboat. We took a winding potholed road down sparsely treed avenues and past brown fields frozen over and mottled in patches of snow. We ran by dark-faced gypsies, wearing denim jackets and slip-ons, pushing old bicycles down the roadside; and we went by long squat houses, beside one of which a bow-legged old woman wrapped in a black shawl swung an axe amid puffs of woodchip and white breath.

"This László Nagy," Timea shouted over the bee-in-a-biscuit-tin hum of the Trabat. "He's something of a local celebrity."

She told me how he would cycle round the high roads and byroads of the plain, pedalling up silently behind people walking down the road, then fire off a starting pistol in their ear – laughing wickedly as they jumped in the ditch or clutched their hearts. That was, until he burst the eardrums of the local police chief whose car had broken down, and who was going for help. He spent a week in the jail as well as the local newspaper for it.

"My dad says that on a fine day he still does it."

"Why?" I asked.

"No one knows. He's a bit of an eccentric. But, of course, you English love that."

Before I could quash this myth, Timea had turned hard left just after a small cement factory, and was now rattling down a dirt track following two ruts across a frozen marsh.

"My father says he lives here," she said, pulling up in front of a low whitewashed building with a wooden veranda running along the front of it, hung with strings of dried green and red peppers and sheaves of herbs. Hens strutted about the compacted bare earth and an obligatory scrawny mongrel yapped at us, straining at its chain, as we got out of the car. The door to the house opened and László Nagy stepped out.

He could have been a matinée idol, a silvery handsome Magyar with sleek grey hair and fine, high cheekbones. He came off the veranda and greeted us a bit warily. He was softly spoken, wrapped in a chunky brown cardigan, avuncular yet shy. He took us round the side of the house down a concrete path past a small allotment. What caught my eye then, and unnerved me, was the macabre forest of dolls' fleshtone body parts and bald chubby heads impaled on canes, along with a plastic yellow duck and green dinosaur, planted among the neat rows of beans and cabbages. It looked like an exploded nursery.

"They keep the birds off," László explained. "Gifts from the Tisza." And he let out a startling burst of laughter.

It was only then that I noticed the huge turbulent expanse of grey-brown water that swept sluggishly, strongly behind the house, carrying with it as it went old fence posts, severed branches and oil cans. For a moment recalling Fortune's story, I peered to see that there was no bathtub moored among the bulrushes. We went into the house, taking our shoes off as we entered. Timea had told him why we had come. Again he gave a rat-a-tat of sudden, loud laughter like a man who isn't used to laughing or to company.

"Me, a film star," he said, "that's a good one."

We sat on a low sofa with an embroidered wrap thrown over it while he put out nuts and saltsticks on a small coffee table before us and poured us glasses of frothy, iodine-yellow beer. He pulled up a carved chair.

"Na," he said. "In 1956 I was anything but a film star." And he went on to tell me, mostly via Timea, how he had been a young Law lecturer at Miskolc university when the Soviet tanks rolled in. He was rounded up with the rest of his colleagues, the dangerous intellectuals of Hungary's so-called "counter-revolution." They were detained in a school hall, forced to sit on their hands, watched over by chain-smoking fresh-faced teenagers casually slung with semi-automatic rifles, who spoke only Russian. It was all a bit unreal, he said. They weren't treated badly but he was young and wanted to escape and go to Budapest. So he said that when it was his turn to be escorted singly to the toilets, he simply scarpered down a long corridor, his fast breath and footsteps echoing off the close walls. He heard a shout and then a shot. But he felt nothing, and carried on running. Looking back briefly at the end of the corridor, he saw that the teenagers had dissolved in laughter, pointing at his escort who had fired a warning shot into the ceiling and was now powdered in white plaster like Buster Keaton in flour. It took him three days, he said, to get to Budapest, mainly by hitching lifts from tractors and scooters. All the cars were loaded to the roof with children and belongings, streaming past him towards the Austrian border.

He got to Budapest, he said, and was sickened by the devastation. There was rubble and massive iron stars thrown down in the streets, and all the shop windows were smashed. But there was no looting, he said. He was very proud of that. And people still formed queues for bread and meat.

László then fell dreadfully quiet. Tears welled in his eyes, the events of forty-odd years ago spilling hotly into the peaceable present. Softly he said that on his first morning in Budapest he saw a queue of elderly women outside a baker's get strafed by Soviet machine gun fire, and crumple where they stood, among smashed eggs, spilled loaves and baskets. They bled so much, he said, calling all the time for husbands and sons. He was incensed and immediately demanded a gun. He was given a pistol. It was only after his first encounter with secret service AVO snipers that he realized it was a starting pistol. Among chipped plaster and spurting tarmac, he stood futilely shooting blanks at an unseen enemy. In fact, the only AVO man he did see was already dead. A corpse flash-fried in petrol and hung from a lamp post with a sign round its neck reading: *Így jár minden AVO* – this is what happens to all AVO. The smell of charred flesh and singed hair made him gag and turn away. It was a smell which eventually made him return home, only for it to seep into his dreams for years to come, choking them with its porky reek.

But it wasn't the AVO man that gave him these nightmares; it was the memory of a young girl whose car had been hit by a Soviet shell. She had somehow managed to free herself from the wreckage but her long gabardine and blond hair had caught fire, were ablaze. László and others ran to her but a spray of bullets drove them back. So they watched helplessly as she pirouetted in the street, whirling the flames higher, so they licked off her lips and eyelids before she collapsed, smouldering a while there, in the empty rubble-strewn Parisian-style boulevard, like a patch of tar. He walked out of Budapest that night, moving against the thick river of traffic and people going the other way.

A week later, he said, he was back in Tiszalök. Party officals came to pick him up on Christmas day. He was still living with his parents, and his mother stuffed cold sausage and peppers into his pockets, sobbing "Laci, Laci," as they lowered his head into the back seat of the car. It was the last time he saw his parents alive. They died while he was in prison; he wasn't allowed out for the funerals. Eight years, he said, he spent in prison, during which time he avenged himself as best he could against the huge iron machine of state. He and other lecturers were set to work translating texts from German, mostly eulogies of Marx.

"Marx and his faithful wife Engels…" he said wistfully. And he shook his head then, interrupting our laughter. He had got a beating and two broken ribs, followed by two weeks solitary confinement for that translation.

"So what did you do when you got out?" I asked him.

"Return home," he said. "Here. I also bought two cats and named them after my parents. Jáncsi and Miska. Then

110

I grew vegetables, bought some hens." There was a pause. "I also keep my bicycle well-oiled," rapping out another machine-gun burst of laughter.

Timea asked him about the river, if he used it for anything. He just huffed.

"My mother used to wash our clothes in it, slamming them dry against great flat stones, but now if I did that I'd lose my hands or they'd all come out bleached. It's polluted. TVK."

I thought this was a kind of pesticide.

"Tisza Vegyi Kombinát," he explained. The chemical works built outside Tiszaújváros which, along with the powerstation, employed almost all of the town. Even by the standards of this bleak industrial hinterland, it was a giant plant, miles across, seething with steam and noxious fumes, with thick silver pipes and towering grimy stacks. Its row of chimneys, which László called Stalin's ducks, pulsed and pumped out a different colour of skyline every day, usually in purples and oranges. Curiously enough, their palette of colours was matched almost exactly by that of the older town women's hairdos, their rust-orange or purple rinses perched fluffily on lined, hard faces usually puckered up like a cat's bum about a "Worker's" cigarette.

László told us that there was a field directly behind and downward of the chemical works which was littered with dead birds, with crows and starlings mostly, that had flown through the reek pouring out of the chimneys and died instantly. Sometimes rarer birds, flocks of geese and finches, plummeted out of an apparently harmless sky.

"It used to be worse," he said, "before they fitted the new filters."

Then it snowed black. Black snow fell, and people's skin itched or erupted in rashes. The river water, László said, would probably do the same thing, especially as

111

industrial barges churned up the Tisza's grey-brown waters more and more frequently. So, no, he didn't use the river. Although he added that some people canoed its length, from border to border, from Slovakia to Serbia – or as he put it, "you set off from one cheating Slav and you stop when you see the next."

"Can't you fish in it?" I asked naïvely.

This was greeted with another blast of laughter. He tapped his forehead. "Mad."

"So you don't fish?"

"Yes. But not in there, not in that filthy sewer."

He fished in a canal just outside of Tiszavasvári; the fact that this town was in turn home to the Alkaloida chemical works didn't seem at all contradictory or troublesome to him. He cycled there, he said, grinning. He only caught dirty water fish: catfish, roach and eels. Hundreds of eels, he said. Of course, he didn't eat them himself. No, he chopped them up and fed them to his cats. Something in the way he said it made my scalp tingle and shrink.

"And, you know, the geese too sometimes come off the river and try to get them, right out of the cats' dish."

I began to sweat, and my hands trembled.

"The collared geese?"

He laughed. "I don't know about that. Just geese."

"What's a collared goose?" Timea asked.

"Oh, nothing." I just wanted to leave.

"Yeah," said László suddenly. "Now I remember. He was English too."

"Who was?" asked Timea.

"There was this funny guy, skinny, blond, who came here not so long back and he asked exactly the same question, about geese and things."

I had stood up to go but now found myself laughing, laughing uncontrollably, carelessly. I laughed so hard that

112

tears came to my eyes.

"The bastard," I cried. "The bastard!"

DAVID M^CCALLAM

The Ascension of the Beasts

Unlike the older employees of the New World Aquarium, I had not yet begun to resemble the fish I worked with. In fact I looked, according to my sister Letty, more like a cocker spaniel because of the way I wore my hair, in two thick ponytails sprouting like puffy cinnamon-colored ears from either side of my head. I had worn it like this since I was six, and I didn't listen to Letty, who said it was a ridiculous, childish affectation for anyone over twelve, and only women with perfect features could get away with wearing their hair in non-standard ways. I didn't much care if I looked ridiculous to other people, as I didn't usually think about them.

I wore my hair in two ponytails because that was how my mother fixed it on the first day of first grade. She parted it in the center, scraping the pointed corner of a comb from my forehead to the very back of my skull, as if scalping me. It hurt, as you would expect a scalping to hurt, but the part was perfect: narrow and white and unwavering. Then she took the right half of the hair and pulled it sideways, pulled my scalp so tight that tears came into my eyes, and gathered the hair just above my ear, and I handed her the cloth-covered rubber band and she pulled the hair through, and twisted the band, and pulled the hair through again, and twisted, and pulled again a third time, and this time the band was so stretched out and full of hair that she had to struggle to get it all through – My goodness, Bridget, you have so much hair! – but in the end, when she was done, it was perfect. The hair above the band lay perfectly flat, with none of the little raised furrows I ended up with when I tried to do my own hair. And then she did the same for the other side. And she said, Now you look like a regular little schoolgirl, and took a picture of me, which I still have. I am standing in front of the house grinning, with a front tooth missing, holding my plastic Pink Panther lunch box, and wearing a green dress and blue tennis shoes and yellow socks pulled up to my knees, for although my mother did my hair she let me choose my own clothes. And because she disappeared soon afterwards I always wore my hair that way, to remember her by.

My first job at the Aquarium was tending the four-footed fish in the Exotic Life exhibit. Because they were the main attraction, they lived in a long, low, free-standing glass tank in the middle of the drafty hexagonal room. Five walls of the room were lined with glass tanks full of other exotic fish, and the sixth side opened onto the main lobby of the aquarium.

The four-footed fish looked more like a cross between a stingray and a turtle than any ordinary finned-and-scaly fish. Their bodies were wide and semi-translucent, gray on the outside with the hint of a glowing pink center. Instead of fins they had four splayed, flat vestigial feet. Like stingrays they moved by rippling, but slowly because they were fleshy and thick-bodied. On either side of their heads were enormous eyes covered with a thick film, the round black pupils perfectly centered in yellow irises. They had smooth flesh, free of scales and encased always in clear slime.

The four-footed fish were native to the Great Barrier Reef of Australia and did not flourish outside their natural environment. In spite of lavish care they died often and without provocation. Two or three mornings a week I would arrive at work to find a bloated corpse bobbing on the surface of the water and the remaining live fish huddled reproachfully in a corner of the tank. At any one time there were between four and seven fish living in the tank; shipments arrived every other week to replace the dead.

I stood all day by the tank watching over them as a mother hovers over her ailing infant. I fed them on schedule and cleaned their tank obsessively, scrubbing away algae and scooping up excrement as soon as it appeared. Once a day I changed their water, transferring them temporarily to a smaller tank. They were heavy and so slimy and wriggling that they sometimes slipped from my grasp and fell gasping and flailing to the floor.

In general I don't much care for fish, but for these I harbored inexplicably tender feelings. The maternal affection that made me tremble when I held them squirming and flopping in my arms could not, I think, have been stronger had they been my own offspring. The glowing pink center of their bodies was like a precious gift, long awaited but never expected. That they continued to die, no matter how religiously I tended them, made me feel miserable and contaminated.

Nevertheless I believed that the fish understood and trusted me. Sometimes I found them staring at me through the glass wall of the tank, looking right into my eyes, and I needed no more proof than this of their fundamental humanity.

One night as I was taking a shower (I always came home from work with dried slime all over my arms, face and hair) I noticed a long red scratch on the inside of my forearm. I couldn't remember having cut myself on anything and forgot about it as soon as it disappeared inside my pajama sleeve.

The next day, however, I discovered the cause of the scratch. The fish were growing claws! On the tips of their flat stumpy feet were the tiny beginnings of sharp nails. I

117

worried that they had contracted a new disease, but as the days passed and none of them died I was less concerned. No doubt they were simply entering a new phase in their life-cycle which I had not as yet observed because their predecessors had all died in their youth.

When the claws were a quarter of an inch long, a new stage in their transformation began: they broke out in bumps all over their smooth slimy bodies. This time I panicked and called the fish doctor, who listened to their heartbeats, took urine samples, and assured me that the bumps were merely a form of fish acne, nothing to worry about.

The fish, sensing my dislike of this doctor, proved him wrong the next day. Out of the bumps sprouted the first wiry stubble that soon grew into thick brown prickles. Two weeks from the time they began to grow nails, the four-footed fish were no longer recognizable as fish. The vestigial feet sprouted into paws, the gills closed up, the large eyes receded somewhat, and the flat faces grew into delicate pointed snouts. They now resembled nothing more than little hedgehogs. I had to drain the water from their tank so they wouldn't drown.

They developed the habit of yipping all day long in high-pitched voices as they raced around the tank, thus attracting the attention of numerous children who wanted to pet them. The children's parents were not happy with the changed exhibit because this was an aquarium, and they were here to see aquatic life, not hedgehogs.

The yipping also attracted the attention of the administration, and I received a visit from the director herself, who demanded to know why land animals were living in one of the fish tanks.

I explained that the hedgehogs had evolved from the four-footed fish native to the Great Barrier Reef.

"We don't keep terrestrial mammals in the Aquarium!" bellowed the director, her fish-like eyes bulging even more than usual.

"Shall I call the Zoo?" I asked. "They might need some extra hedgehogs."

"The Zoo? The *Zoo*? Do you know how I feel about the Zoo?"

"No." I stepped back out of reach of her waving arms.

"The Zoo is our enemy!" she shouted. "They steal our business, our tourists, our funding. If it weren't for the Zoo we would be rich, we would be able to afford sharks! Do you know what it would do for our publicity if we had sharks here?"

"Not really."

"Well nobody's calling any goddamn Zoo and giving them free animals. Do you understand?"

If I had been a hedgehog I would've bulldozed her with my spikes. I said, "Shall we just keep them here then?"

"I said that we don't keep terrestrial mammals in the Aquarium, you idiot! Who gave you this job anyway? Are you a spy for the Zoo?"

That was enough. "You will not speak to me in that way," I said. "I do good work here, and you will treat me with respect. Your insulting, histrionic behavior reflects poorly on you and on this institution, and I expect an apology."

She fired me and sent for a janitor to dispose of the hedgehogs. I could not allow them to be thrown out like garbage, so I scooped them into a brown paper grocery bag and went on my way. I was afraid the security guard at the door would stop me when he heard the scrabbling noises from inside the bag, but he was talking to someone on his radio and noticed nothing.

*

119

As a matter of principle I shared my house with no one, not even plants, but I did not hesitate to take in the hedgehogs. They needed me, they were alone in the world, and for once I would make an exception.

There were five at this point, five yipping hedgehogs. I made them a bed in the big cardboard box the TV had come in, using old towels for padding. I knelt on the carpet and peered eagerly into the box, as a hungry shark peers up at a fat piglet about to be tossed into the ocean. Now that they were mine forever I realized that this was what I had always wanted, this ownership, for as long as I had known them, and maybe even before that. I wanted to squeeze them together in a bundle against my chest until they popped. When it was well past midnight and they showed no signs of quieting down for the night, I tried to soothe them by stroking their fur, but whenever I reached into the box they became tremendously excited and dashed around madly, throwing themselves against the cardboard walls of their pen. Their prickles were sharp, and before I knew it my fingertips were covered in blood. I had to put on rubber dishwashing gloves for protection.

I was just as agitated as they were and wanted nothing more than to let them out of the box so I could play with them all night long. As a responsible adult, however, I knew that both they and I needed a good night's sleep, and that they would still be there in the morning.

At last, shortly before dawn, they wore themselves out and fell asleep in a cluster of spiky balls. I slept too, on the carpet beside the box, listening to their quick panting breaths.

They woke me at nine with their yipping. I looked into the box and discovered that one or more of them had excreted a pile of dung balls which they were all rolling

120

around in delightedly. Though disgusted I was used to cleaning up after them, and I took them one by one from the box and bathed them in the bathroom sink, rinsing their soiled coats. I discovered that their underbellies were free of spikes and covered instead with soft white fur. I tickled one and he rolled up into a ball. When they were all clean I let them run loose around the house while I went to the corner store to buy a litterbox and some canned cat food.

And so began a new era in my life. The hedgehogs were a lot of trouble to take care of, even more than they had been as fish, and I soon entered a state of constant exhaustion. My body felt heavy and slow, and the rest of the world seemed far away, muffled, as though behind a thick pane of glass. At the Aquarium – for I wasn't really fired; the assistant director called the very next day and asked me to come back – standing idle at my new post in the tropical fish room, I would stare into the tanks and let my vision blur until all I saw were iridescent blobs of vibrant color – jade, gold, magenta, silvery blue – darting gracefully over a calm aquamarine canvas. Mesmerized, I felt my limbs simultaneously sinking and floating, and then the air split open to reveal, beneath the bustling noise of the aquarium, a deep fuzzy silence, like radio static, which pulled me down and swallowed me, so that I too was made up of dense wavering gray lines, and released me only when a particularly jarring noise intruded from the outside.

I was exhausted largely because the hedgehogs turned out to be nocturnal creatures, in the daytime sleeping as soundly as prehistoric ants frozen in amber, and then yipping and playing all night long. I took to sleeping with earplugs, a noisy fan blowing, and two pillows over my head to muffle the high-pitched sound of their voices, but, although these devices effectively screened out traffic noise and the parties next door, they did not block out – indeed, merely isolated and framed – the hedgehogs' shrill irregular yipping and squealing. I fell asleep only when I was able to seek out and fall into that vast roar of static lying in wait beneath all the other noise.

But in spite of the inconvenience I felt a deep joy at having them in my home. I had always treasured the peace and independence of solitary living, but I soon welcomed the feeling I got every evening coming home to a houseful of newly-awakened, energetic, affectionate hedgehogs. They couldn't stay away from me. Whenever I walked by they attacked my dolphin slippers and climbed up the legs of my sweatpants, digging their little claws through the soft knit fabric into my flesh. Sometimes I cooked dinner with two or three of them clinging to my legs the whole time. When I watched TV they crawled onto the couch, sat in my lap, and burrowed their snouts in the crook of my elbow. I had never been needed before, and the sensation was intoxicating. I finally understood why Letty went to such lengths to keep me as her "little" sister, why she always tried to find some reason to feel sorry for me and comfort me: it made her feel big and strong and warm, as I did during a thunderstorm when all the hedgehogs piled into my lap and trembled with fear.

They were smart, too, and soon learned to play several games: hide-and-seek (I was always It); fetch, with tiny red bouncing balls; and bowling, their favorite, in which they curled up into prickly balls and I rolled them across the floor at high speeds. When they wanted to play they ran around behind me and nipped at my heels until I obliged them with a game.

Above all else they loved boxes. Five shoe boxes filled

with cedar shavings became their beds, and larger cardboard boxes scattered through the house were the caverns where they hid from me when we played hide-and-seek or when they were sulking. I also made them an elaborate cardboard castle with multiple levels, cut-out windows, and Kleenex-box furniture, which provided extra hiding places within the larger structure.

Although their appetites were hearty they were finicky. After weeks of experimentation I discovered that their favorite meal was moist liver-flavored cat food mixed with tomato paste in the precise proportion of three to one, though because the cat food was expensive I sometimes made it two to one and hoped they wouldn't make a fuss.

Sometimes, when they were making too much noise for me to sleep, I put them all together in a box in the backseat of the car and went for long midnight drives. I drove on the interstate out of the city into the country, where there were no street lamps over the highway, and all I could see were the shadowy trees whisking past on the side of the road, the white beam of the headlights pushing weakly against the blackness ahead, the bright green exit signs with reflecting silver letters, and the sky as dark as the deepest depths of the ocean. I was at peace on these drives, and not at all lonely, though apart from the truck drivers I was the only person awake for miles and miles. My turbulent thoughts were soothed by the regular flow of objects from ahead to behind, and my mind became a void, detached from past and future. The world flew by my windows, but I remained still and quiet at the center.

The motion of the car put the hedgehogs to sleep, and when we got home I could usually enjoy a few hours of quiet before they woke up again.

It occurred to me before long that I was becoming soft. I put up with disturbances from the hedgehogs that I never would have tolerated from any human beings living in my house. But, really, what else could I do?

On Thursday nights I went over to Letty's house to watch TV. She and her husband Grant were the only family I had left, and they were kind to me, though they constantly nagged at me to "get out and see the world" and "live a little." I didn't mind not having any other friends, but they minded for me. I was a puzzle to them, perhaps even a joke: antisocial, private to the point of prickliness, perverse about my hairstyle. A puzzle, not a person.

But I enjoyed those Thursday nights. Grant cooked dinner and served it to us in the living room. We ate watching TV with our plates balanced on our knees. Letty talked constantly during the programs, commenting on the actors' hairstyles and dress and acting ability, and Grant and I begged her to hush, but we didn't really mind. I sometimes wished I was their child, so I could stay always in their house, and be fed and taken care of by two loving parents.

After our mother disappeared Letty raised me, though she was only three years older than I. My father was there, of course, but he and I did not know how to talk to each other without Letty as an intermediary. At dinner every night he would ask me, "So, girl, whaddaya know?" and I would mumble, "Not much," and stare down at my plate, letting my hair hang in front of my face to hide my embarrassment, and then Letty would jump in to hide my inadequacy with "Guess what, Dad, Bridget got a hundred on her spelling test today!" or "Did you know that Bridget's going out for the track team tomorrow? Isn't that something!" She could afford to be generous in her praise of me, for she knew he much preferred her. And I was grateful to her for protecting me in this way, though I also resented her, more and more as time went on. If she hadn't been there I might have learned to speak for myself; I might have known my father.

Letty was only a couple of inches shorter than I, but that little bit made all the difference in the world. I outgrew her when I was thirteen, and, at the same time as I began to look down on her, I also began to see that she was not as big and strong and wise as I had thought; she had faults; she was fragile in a way I had never noticed before. Her shoulders, seen from above, were narrow and frail. She did not really know what to make of our father, any more than I did. Her bright chirping dinner talk was nothing but a fragile eggshell hiding... what? Fear, insecurity, loneliness? I never asked her. We both became aware, during my adolescence, of how little we knew each other. Because I never said what I was feeling, Letty thought me cold. Because she blurted out her feelings to anyone and everyone she met, I thought them common and shallow, the kind of feelings you could read in any tabloid or trash novel, unlike mine, which I dared not loose upon the world for fear of the havoc they would wreak. For a while I had nothing but contempt for her, but by my late teens, when she graduated from college and married Grant, I was more tolerant, and no longer believed I could "see through" her, though I suspected she was much more calculating than she let on about her effect on other people.

But when I came to know Grant, and understood what a great man he was, all my negative opinions of Letty vanished forever. I saw that he would never have chosen to spend the rest of his life with someone less great than he, and when I looked for evidence of Letty's greatness I found it in abundance. I wondered how I had never noticed that she was perfect. She was like an old quilt I'd had on my bed for so many years that I stopped noticing its beautiful patterns. All I cared about was that it kept me warm at night, and I didn't treat it well. I lay with my shoes on the bed, spilled food on it, and picked at the threads when I was nervous. And then one day someone came into my room and saw it for the first time and said, "What a beautiful quilt! It belongs in a museum!" and pointed out to me the vibrant colors, the fine cloth of the patches, the intricate pattern, the small, even stitches. And because he appreciated the quilt so much more than I did he took it away to his own room – for wouldn't an ordinary blanket serve me just as well? – and hung it on his wall, for all to admire. And I was ashamed that I had not realized before that the quilt was for art, not for living with.

Letty was warm and loving, laughed often and beautifully, listened intelligently, looked good at cocktail parties. Even her faults – a tendency to make inane comments about subjects of which she knew nothing, for instance, or her habit of talking during movies – only made her more endearing. In fact, she could not go wrong; she was blessed with a manner that made everything right. I think I fell in love with her as much as Grant did. Even her name, Letitia, Letty, which I had never much liked, revealed new depths of meaning. Letitia was soft, delicate, fluttering, a lace handkerchief falling through the air. Letty was sweet and flippant, a daytime name, a young person's name, a bouquet of daisies tossed on the bed. Why had my parents not named me Letty and her Bridget? Then everything might have been different.

I had to struggle to keep myself from mimicking every aspect of her behavior. As tempting as it was, I reasoned that Grant would have no incentive to leave her for me if I were her clone, and I could only make that happen by being perfectly myself, more perfectly Bridget than she was

126

Letty. Not that I would ever in reality have stolen him away from her; I had too much self-respect for that; but it was a nice thought, sometimes, all the time really, when I was alone.

I didn't like to use the word "love" about my feeling for him. It was too common, too small a word for this vast turbulence inside me, and besides, my feeling would never, could never, have a happy ending. I wanted a word like elephantiasis or poltergeist or Saskatchewan, a word with power and music and anger, and some hint of bedevilment. I wanted a word that meant, "I rend and am rent; I flay and am flayed; I smash and am smashed." I was furious, not at Letty but at Grant, because he did not see me. He pulled my ponytails, treated me like a kid sister, but did not really look at me.

I would have beat him senseless if it would've made him see me.

Of course I could never say how I felt; it wouldn't have been right; so I kept it to myself and was quietly miserable.

After two months the hedgehogs began to shed their prickles in great numbers. I had to wear hard-soled shoes around the house because the prickles buried in the carpet slid easily through the cloth of my socks and slippers to pierce my feet. I tried to vacuum them up, but they made a terrible clatter inside the vacuum cleaner, and I resorted to crawling around on the carpet on my knees, gathering them by hand as I went. In place of the prickles the hedgehogs grew thick brown hair, long and silky like a spaniel's.

All this time they were growing rapidly. After three months they were the size of small terriers, and when they tried to climb up my legs they ripped long tears in my pants. Their appetites increased, their voices became deeper and rougher, and their legs lengthened. I knew that they would soon outgrow my tiny house, but because so much of my earnings went to pay for their food I couldn't afford to move to a bigger place. As they grew they became less active and spent most of the day and night lying on the carpet watching TV. I was pleased that they were settling down but sorry they no longer paid so much attention to me, and sorry, too, that they were no longer little and cuddly.

By November, the fifth month since I'd brought them home, they had grown so tall that the tops of their heads came up to my waist. Their legs were gangly and lightly-furred, their paws had long dexterous toes, and distinct necks now divided their heads from their bodies; in the fish and hedgehog stages they'd had no necks to speak of. Their snouts receded somewhat, so that they looked a little like pug-nosed terriers.

As they grew they became less and less interested in me, and my affection for them became at once more desperate and less pleasurable. They began to seem more of a burden, even though they were not as intrusive and rambunctious as they had been when they were smaller. I spent most of my evenings feeding, grooming, and cleaning up after them, yet they showed no gratitude at all: no cheerful licks on my cheek, no little snouts nuzzling my hands for attention. They acted aloof and self-sufficient, though I knew they wouldn't last a week without me.

Although their new personalities did not please me, I still delighted in watching them. The movements of their new bodies were delicate and springy. They trotted rather than walked, lifting their large paws daintily. In spite of their voracious eating they were thin, and I loved to watch the muscles and bones moving smoothly under their glossy brown coats. When they lay on the floor watching TV, I sat on the couch behind them and stared not at the TV but at them. The fact of their breath seemed a miracle. I was mesmerized by the rise and fall of their rib cages. How did they know how to breathe so well?

At night I let them out into the backyard and watched them run and play in the moonlight. Just as on the midnight drives, I felt that I was opening up, becoming more aware of the world. I am here, I am here, I thought sometimes, feeling all of a sudden, as I stood barefoot in the cool grass, droplets of water from the sprinkler next door, flung by the breeze over the high wooden fence to land on my face and bare arms. And then I felt breathless, as though I'd been running for a train and had only just caught it, and now I was sitting back in my seat watching the beautiful new scenery rush past and still feeling frightened at the thought that I could so easily have missed seeing this world, the real world, of plants and animals and physical objects, and would have been caught forever in the shifting, ambiguous, frustrating world of people. Weather and oceans and fresh smells after rain: these things were worth reveling in. Watching the dogs, I felt connected to the earth.

But I was also troubled: I am here, and it is beautiful, but what do I do?

One night the doorbell rang.

"Who could that be?" I asked in a tone of exaggerated enthusiasm. With the animals I had developed the habit of speaking aloud to no one in particular, narrating my actions as if they were somehow exceptional. The dogs glanced over at me, but quickly returned their attention to the TV screen.

I looked through the keyhole and saw Grant standing on the porch. I stopped smiling and opened the door.

"Hi," I said tentatively, but did not move out of the doorway.

He was still dressed in a suit and tie; he must've come straight from work.

"Can I come in?" he asked with a smile, as if this was just the sort of inhospitable welcome he'd been expecting, and it amused him.

"Is Letty okay?" I asked.

"Oh yes," he said. "I just stopped by on my way home from work to see how you're getting along. We haven't had much of a chance to talk lately."

I moved out of the doorway and let him in, but I was puzzled. Stopped by? No one ever "stopped by" to see me, partly because everyone knew I wouldn't like it – I didn't usually let other people into my house – and partly because I didn't really know anyone, apart from Letty and Grant, and I always went over to their house.

He sat on the couch. "Wow, you've got dogs!" he said. "You didn't tell us you had dogs."

"They haven't been dogs for long," I said.

He gave me a strange smile, the smile you give to a madman to humor him so he won't chop you up into little bits with his butter knife. "They're very nice dogs," he said. "What breed?"

"I'm not sure," I said. "I found them."

We sat there a moment, looking at the dogs.

"Can I get you something to eat?"

"Sure, I'm starved. What've you got?"

"How about some moist liver-flavored cat food mixed with tomato paste?"

"Excuse me?" He didn't see that it was a joke.

"It's what I feed the hedgehogs," I said. "I mean the dogs."

"Ah, I see." He smiled. "Do you have any people food? Or drink?"

"Orange juice?"

"That will be splendid." He settled back on the couch and I went to get the juice. Why was it, I wondered, that when I was alone I seemed perfectly normal, but when I had to speak to someone I became a strange, bumbling, asocial creature and got all the nuances wrong?

But I would try my hardest to impress him. I began to like the idea of having a Guest. I wanted him to have a good time, to come again. I wanted to talk to him, to tell him the things that were important to me, to hear what was important to him. I wanted him to know me. I thought that if he knew me he would probably like me, and that if he liked me I would like myself more. I might even discover that, like Letty, I too was perfect, in my own way.

But why had he come? Perhaps to tell me – but no, I couldn't think of that, not even think it.

"I've never seen you with your hair down before," he said as I handed him the glass of orange juice. "And I'm stunned. You look beautiful."

Me? Beautiful?

He continued. "Why don't you wear it down more often?"

That made me angry. This was no disinterested compliment, but a political maneuver. "Did Letty tell you to say that? She hates the way I wear my hair, but it's none of her business, and none of yours, either."

He raised his eyebrows, uncrossed his legs and crossed them the other way, and stuck his tongue in one corner of his cheek. "Okay," he said. "We'll talk about the weather."

"I'm sorry," I said sullenly. "I'm sensitive about my hair."

"No problem." He waved it away. "Tell me what's on your mind."

That was the wrong thing to say. Too much like my father's dinnertime quiz: "Whaddaya know, girl? Tell me

131

something about yourself. Speak up now."

I sat there, on the other side of the couch. I thought that surely conversations were supposed to be easier than this, or people wouldn't have them.

Nothing was on my mind.

Nothing but the mystery of the fish-turned-hedgehogs-turned dogs, my tearing-and-torn-apart feeling for him, the age-old ache for my mother, the midnight romps in the backyard when nothing more than a sprinkling of water on my face made me feel suddenly alive. But how could I say these things to him?

I could say this: I like to imagine that we are two rabbits, you and I, lying on the cool grass on a June morning. You are a big fat black rabbit and I am a little brown-and-white lop-ear. The grass is still cold and wet from the night, but I am not cold because you are beside me, large and black, exuding warmth. We have had our breakfast and now we sit here wiggling our noses, as rabbits do, watching the world go on around us, good things and bad things, it doesn't matter what happens; we just watch and wiggle our noses. One of your long soft ears falls over my eyes, but I don't push it away. It is warm and smells of clean grass, and the skin is so thin that I can see the light shining through it, and the big thick veins pulsing beneath the velvet fur.

And when the hungry opossum comes gnashing his teeth I will not be afraid, for I know that he will prefer you, the big fat rabbit, to me, the skinny little lop-ear.

It is a terrible thing to live in the middle of the food chain.

I had nothing to say.

I stared down at the dogs, who were still watching TV, though I had muted the sound so I could talk to Grant. I looked up at him and saw that he was watching the TV, too.

I said, desperately, "I like to go outside at night."

He smiled and nodded, indicating that I had done well in my first effort at conversation. "I know that feeling," he said. "In law school my favorite time to study was in the middle of the night, when it was quiet, and no one else was around."

"Yes, it is a good time," I said lamely.

"But you have to be careful where you go at night," he warned. "This is not a safe place for a young woman to be wandering around alone after dark."

He doesn't know me, I thought. He has no idea who I am. I have been deluding myself to think that he saw even a little beyond my awkward manners to who I am when I'm alone.

"Yes," I said. And then I leapt off the cliff. "Why did you come over tonight, really?" I asked. "What did you want to tell me?"

He held up his hands, a bit defensively. "No ulterior motive," he said. "Just a friendly visit."

Why did I think I was in love with this person I couldn't even talk to? None of the thousands of conversation I'd had with him in my head had been the least bit awkward.

I said nothing.

"Well, I guess I'd better be on my way," he said, "or Letty will be worried."

"Okay," I said.

"Thanks for the juice!"

I let him out and locked the door behind him. Then I lay down on the couch, and a hundred-ton pillow settled over my body, smothering me, making escape impossible. I had failed. My one chance to talk to him alone, to impress him somehow, to make a real connection, and I failed. I wanted to cry, scream, tear something up, but I couldn't. The pillow weighed me down. One of the dogs stood up and came over to me. He licked my dry face. I reached out to pet him. "Thank you," I said. "You're the only one who understands."

But he didn't really understand. He ran to the kitchen, whining for his dinner.

I wondered, should I go away? Should I leave this place and these people who torture me so? Every time I saw him I felt terrible afterwards. I went home and cried. Was anyone worth feeling this miserable about? I couldn't say Yes, and I couldn't say No.

The other dogs went into the kitchen and joined the first in whining for food. The hundred-ton pillow vanished and I stood up, light-headed.

When in mid-December the dogs began groaning and rolling around on the floor, I called the vet's office in a panic and made an emergency appointment. But when the time came for me to get them into the car they wouldn't get up off the floor, and I wasn't strong enough to carry them. I spent two hours trying to coax them out the front door. I was terrified, sure they were dying, but eventually they stopped groaning and perked up a little, and a nurse at the vet's assured me over the phone that they would probably be okay until the morning; it sounded like a touch of food poisoning; give them plenty of water but no food until they see the doctor. I went to bed certain that I would wake up to find five dead dogs on my living room floor.

As it happened, the morning revealed a perfectly ordinary explanation for the groaning: growing pains, or rather the pains of metamorphosis. I came out of my bedroom and found the house a shambles. In the kitchen five large apes were standing on the countertop pulling food from the cupboards and throwing it on the floor.

The lethargic phase was over. The apes were smart, wild and malicious. Every day while I was at work they destroyed the house. I had to lock them inside and take all the keys with me so they wouldn't get out into the neighborhood and reveal their presence; I didn't think it was legal to keep endangered animals inside city limits. I was also afraid that, if they got loose, they might attack someone. Often they looked evilly at me from under half-closed eyelids as if they hated and wanted to kill me, but fortunately they seemed to realize that without me they would starve.

I began to hate them for hating me so unjustly. I had given them nothing but care and affection and they took it all for granted. They even seemed contemptuous of me for serving them so faithfully. (Or was it I who was contemptuous of myself for putting up with their ingratitude?) All my free time went to cleaning up their messes, though I knew that if I left the house even for an hour the mess would miraculously reappear, worse than before.

Before this they had always gotten along with one another. Now they became enemies not only of me but of each other. They fought for dominance, hurling objects, charging, shaking the furniture, screaming, grimacing terribly. No single one ever emerged the leader after these displays; they simply grouped together again and united against me.

Not only their behavior but their physical selves repelled me. The wispy hair growing scantily over their bodies was a sad remnant of the once thick and glossy dog hair I had loved. The wrinkled black skin of their faces, the bubble-gum pink mouths, the yellowy-white fuzz under the chin, the arms longer than the legs – it was all grotesque.

Worst of all they were big, four feet tall and as heavy as I was. Only their big brown eyes showed some hint of human kindness, but they lowered their eyelids and blotted it out.

After a month of this I couldn't stand it anymore and called the Zoo. I said I had discovered five apes starving in a dumpster and had brought them home but didn't know what to do with them, and they seemed to be sick, losing hair. Would the Zoo take them off my hands? It would, the following evening at seven. I arrived home at five, looking forward to a peaceful evening for the first time in eight months. But the apes were gone, and in their place, sitting on my couch watching TV, were five hairy naked men.

"Hey, look who's here!" they shouted.

"Did you bring the beer?"

"Don't worry, we already called the Zoo. Told them not to come because the apes died, ha ha."

"You're not getting rid of us yet, Gidget."

"What is this?" I asked, in a daze, wondering how my life could have degenerated so quickly into such a farce.

"We're your friends, Widget, don't you remember us?" They snickered. "By the way, you need to run to the store and grab some beer. The game's about to start."

I backed slowly out the door, locked it, and sat down, stunned, on the porch steps. How could this have happened? Was I supposed to keep taking care of them, now that they were full-grown men, human beings, responsible for their own behavior? How had they learned English? Was this a hoax, a practical joke? And what had happened to my sweet animals?

I sat there for a long time, listening passively to the fragmented shrieks that burst upon my mind like firecrackers. It emerged, eventually, out of the chaos, that this was something remarkable. Perhaps this was my destiny. To raise creatures from fish to human beings, that was a great achievement, a privilege even. I could not abandon them now. I went to get the beer.

They had learned English from watching TV. They spoke with a phony Australian accent, saying it was only fitting, as they had originally come from Australia. They remembered everything that had ever happened to them and everything I had done. They liked to reminisce about my past behavior – "Hey, remember when Midget used to scoop our shit out of the water?" "Yeah, she was really into that stuff, maybe she'd like to wipe my ass now." "How about it, Twidget?"

All they did, all day long, was make fun of me. Anything that made me miserable or hurt my feelings they would do. They refused to wear clothes until I promised that I would let them out into the backyard during the day if they wore shorts, at least. So they sat outside in the sun and tanned dark brown and drank beer and listened to loud music and were rude to the neighbors. They also insisted on coming with me to Letty's house, where, perversely, they were charming.

"Little Bridget's all grown up," said Grant one day, when my "friends" were not there. "Living in a house with five men! I never would've thought it." I liked him least when he was patronizing.

Letty laughed and said, "Five handsome, scantily-clad men with accents!"

I did not like to be mocked, but I could not explain. Who would have believed me?

"Where did they come from?" asked Letty.

"I found them in the Aquarium," I said. "They had nowhere to go, so I brought them home." My sister and her

137

husband exchanged glances.

"You know, Bridget," he said, "you really shouldn't be bringing strangers home like that. I mean, you never know."

"If you wanted to meet men," said Letty, "you should have come with me to the gym."

"I don't like them," I said. "They're rude and messy and I don't know how to make them leave."

"This is your mess, little sister," said Grant, and for a moment I hated him. "We really shouldn't get involved."

"If you want them to leave, you have to assert yourself," said Letty.

"I don't know what to do," I said, desperate for advice. "They needed my help and I helped them, I thought that was the right thing to do, but they don't care, they just want to use my things and eat my food, they don't care about me, but I still don't know if it's right to turn them out." I began to cry.

"Poor little Bridget," said Grant, and hugged me, and I didn't hate him anymore.

"You don't owe them anything," said Letty. "Men! Here, blow your nose."

"I'll tell you what to do," said Grant. "You give them until the end of the week to be out of the house. I'll come over on Saturday morning and make sure they don't give you any trouble about leaving."

"Okay," I sniffed. "Till the end of the week, then."

Saturday came, and they left with a few curses but nothing worse. Grant was there to back me up. After they had gone I called a locksmith and had the locks changed. Grant and Letty stayed all day helping me clean the house, and after they had gone I went to bed, though it was only six o'clock in the evening. I curled up under the blankets and shivered, sensing that something terrible was going to happen to me. The phone was next to the bed; if they came back I could call the police. The shades were down and the room was diffused with a dim gray light. It reminded me of a sickroom, of my mother's room, long ago, where I used to go and lie down after school and pretend that I was sick, and that she was downstairs cooking soup for me and would soon come upstairs and put damp washcloths on my head to ease the fever, and that they had not found her car abandoned in a parking lot, with the windows smashed. I felt that I had been ill, a long illness, and I would be a long time recovering. I needed to close my eyes and forget everything and sleep for months. Soon I was hot under too many blankets but was too tired to pull them off. I woke once when it was dark and saw the five men looking down at me. "Make dinner," they said, but I just laughed and rolled over on my stomach with my face in the pillow, the buttons of my pajama top pressing into my chest. After that it was all a blur, the nights and days rushing past. The hedgehogs were climbing around on my limp body, bouncing gently on my stomach. I laughed, or tried to, but heard only a hoarse croak instead of my voice, and the skin of my face felt tight and strained when I parted my lips to smile. Some made a nest of my hair all spread out behind me on the pillow; some rested on my stomach; others nuzzled my hand and licked my fingers. There seemed to be a great many more of them than there once had been. They would start growing again soon, I knew, into their larger and more horrible versions, but there was nothing I could do about it, I realized, no more running away or shutting them out, because now they had gotten inside my head, and nothing on earth would dislodge them.

And then the phone rang, and I heard their nasty menacing voices, "Come see what we have done," and a dial tone, and I sat up in bed, alert and terrified, for I knew them.

I ran from the house in my pajamas, got in my car and drove barefoot to Letty's house, and when I saw the open front door a red-hot shudder poured down my skin and I wanted to die right there, before I saw anything else.

Letty was not dead, but she lay weakly on the floor. Down her face, neck and arms were a multitude of scratches. The skin around her eyes and lips was swollen. One of her wrists lay at an odd angle. But she was not dead.

She spoke hoarsely when she saw me, cursing the five men, calling for retribution, sobbing. I called 911 and Grant at work and waited with Letty until I heard the sirens in the distance.

"I'll take care of them," I told her, and drove back home, where I knew they'd be waiting.

They were sitting on the porch drinking beer. Instead of giving in to hysterical rage I spoke quietly.

"Get in the car, right now. The police are on their way here and they will beat you to death."

They obeyed and piled into the car, three people to a seat. I drove away, surprised at my own composure, and stopped first at a camping store.

"You," I said to the one beside me. "Come in with me. The rest of you, do not move." I spoke in a low, threatening voice.

Inside the store a salesman fitted the one man out in full mountain garb: long underwear, fleece shirt, Goretex pants and parka, wool socks, hiking boots, ski mask and gloves. I bought five of each item. As I was paying, my wild man came up to me holding a watch. "Look," he said. "It's waterproof and works as deep as three hundred feet underwater!"

I saw the rust-colored stains under his fingernails.

"Can I have it?" he asked.

I looked at him, this large man, so childlike, begging for a toy, so animal-like, my sister's blood still visible on his hands. How had I ever thought I could tame them? And how had I been so foolish as to let them out into civilization?

"If you have a watch," I said, "the others will be jealous. They will tear your arm off to get at it."

"Please," he begged. "Just for me. Not them." I bought it for him.

I drove fast for many hours, westward, over the plains to the mountains, stopping only to refuel. When we reached the wilderness area I had chosen it was 6 AM. I parked beside the trail and they tumbled out into the cold morning.

"Get dressed," I said, taking their new outfits from the trunk. Shivering, they changed clothes. I was still wearing my pajamas, with bare feet, but I forced myself to stand calmly on the cold pebbly ground.

"Listen to me," I said as they dressed. "Don't ever come back. What you did was very bad – you almost killed a woman – and for that they'll put you away for a very long time. You're wild animals, I realize that now, and I never should've tried to keep you shut up with me." They stood there, mute, staring at me, their shoulders sagging.

"Don't leave us here," they begged. "We aren't meant to live in the cold."

"Go." I pointed to the trailhead. "And don't come back, or I'll kill you myself."

They looked at me, and they looked at each other, and then they rushed towards me, to hug me I thought at first, but no, I was falling backwards, a long long way. The ground was impossibly far behind me. I heard the sound of my head striking the earth, and then there was a purple blob of pain and endless rough movement. The next thing I understood was an impossible cold, the sharpest most painful cold imaginable. I understood that I could not breathe, that I was in the water, that I was drowning.

I struggled, but not so much against the drowning as against the cold. Breathing would be nice but most important was getting out of the terrible freezing water. They held me down, and I struggled up once or twice for air, but really I had no chance. It was five big men against one small woman. At the last moment I made a choice, I really did, though you may find it hard to believe. I chose to breathe, not to drown. I stopped struggling and took a deep breath and filled my lungs with water. I won't say it wasn't uncomfortable at first – I thought I was dying – but I soon realized that it was the first real breath of my life. The clean cold alpine water rushed into my lungs and brain and heart and woke me up. The only thing I can compare it to is the sensation of coming out of a bar, disgusted by the stink of cigarette smoke and spilt beer and sweaty bodies, stepping outside into the night and taking a deep breath of sharp December air and washing all the dirtiness out of your lungs. That was how it felt, my first breath of water.

The men were surprised, I think, at how easily I shook them off. Certainly they let go after a few powerful swishes of my muscular tail. As I swam away I looked back and saw the five pairs of legs still standing in the water. That was my last glimpse of them. Then I dove way down to the bottom of the lake, far below the floating icebergs, to the deepest mud.

It is warm, down here in the mud, where I spend my nights. Even the water isn't that cold once you get used to it. The other fish leave me alone, for I am still five-and-a-half feet long, average for a woman but very big for a fish.

I don't know what kind of fish I am. I try to turn my head to see the rest of my body, but it's difficult without a neck. Sometimes I leap up into the air and look down at my reflection in the water. I think I am a silvery blue color. I'm still waiting for my instincts to kick in and tell me what to do, what to eat, how to interact with the other fish. For now I eat water bugs and minnows, as there's really nothing else. I used to think that fish were incredibly dumb to fall for the old worm-on-a-hook trick, but the truth is that the sight of a juicy squirming nightcrawler after nothing but water bugs and minnows for six months is enough to make anyone lose his head. I try to resist the temptation, though I flatter myself that I am too clever to be caught.

This is a silent wavering world. The dark slimy lake plants wave gently to and fro, and we fish slink and weave noiselessly among them, not speaking, not looking directly at one another. From time to time we hear a small plop or splash from the surface, when someone catches a minnow or jumps for a flying insect. I jump and splash more than most and get odd looks for it. I don't think they quite approve of me. I also spend a lot of time looking up at the sun, a soft distorted version of the one you see outside. Someone has popped the yolk and the yellow spills out into the rest of the sky. In the mornings and evenings the lake lies under the shadow of the mountains on either side, but at midday the sunlight breaks through and casts long slanting greeny-blue streaks of light through the dark water.

I watch the sun for long periods, trying to make sense of its shape, and as I watch I hear my mother's voice saying, Don't stare at the sun, you'll burn your eyes out, and I hear my father's and my sister's voices saying, You'll burn your eyes out, burn your eyes out, but for once in my life I feel immeasurably distant from my family and their concerns and admonitions. After everything else that has happened, the prospect of burning my eyes out does not much worry me.

I will not stay down here forever. I chose to be a fish, and when I'm ready I'll choose to go back up again, into the real world where shapes and sounds are hard and definite, and the sun does not break up into a bright wobbling jelly. But for now I have years' and years' worth of thoughts to think through. I will go back someday, but not until I'm ready.

HILLARY STEVENS

The Coffee Habit

This morning, like every morning, my coffee beans said to me, "You can take it, no problem."

"Nooo..." I moaned, hiding under my double duvet. "I'm sleeping."

"Up and at 'em!" said the beans, shiny brown and unctuous in their packet.

"I'm sleeping alone," I lamented, "so you can leave me alone too."

"Well, now you're waking up alone," said the beans, who'd heard it all before, "so come and join us instead. Never say die, it's a beautiful morning."

"It's a horrible morning," I said, rolling out of bed and curling up on the floor. "It's raining."

"Pennies from heaven," said the beans. "Upsadaisy."

I shoved myself upright and crossed over to my cappuccino maker on my knees.

"That's the spirit!" said the beans. "Nearly there, come on, you can make it!"

I took hold of the packet, three-quarters full of smooth-roasted cheerleaders all chanting "That's the spirit! That's the spirit!" I poured some of them into the grinder to shut them up, and switched it on. Even over the roar of the blade, I could hear them, still chanting "Go for it! Go for it!" their voices getting squeakier as they got ground into smaller and smaller bits.

"I'm only making coffee for one now," I sighed to them. "No Joseph to wake up to." The ground beans had gone too high-pitched for me to hear them – maybe I should get a dog to translate for me, dogs can hear high sounds – but the remaining beans twinkled at me in their aromatic way.

"All the more for you, eh?" they told me.

I stroked the cappuccino maker, the present from Joseph. Grounds in one bit, water in another, and it sorts my life out for me. "See?" said the beans. "The cappuccino maker still loves you."

"Cheers," I mumbled, leaning my sleepy head against the wall and switching it on. "Doesn't bring me flowers, does it?"

"Who needs flowers when you've got your health?" the caffeine-laden little carcinogens yelled over the noise of the machine.

"You don't talk sense," I told them. "And you're smug and I'm sleepy, and furthermore the man who introduced me to coffee in the first place has dumped me and I'm about to drink some of your relations. Doesn't any of that *bother* you?"

"Plenty more fish in the sea," they told me.

"No, no, I mean doesn't it bother you that I'm about to drink your kinsfolk?" The cappuccino machine presented me with a frothing, scented cup as a token of its regard for me.

"Best place for them, really," they shrugged.

"How can it not bother you?"

I'm definitely going to get a dog, I decided. I'll get a nice dog to cuddle up to at night, and it can translate the grounds for me. It'll tell me what they *really* think about being drunk. I bet those beans already know, but they won't tell me. They're up to something, I know it. But I'll show them, cheerful little bastards. I'll get a dog and he'll translate for me, and then we'll see what's what.

And if it comes to that, how can the little toadies be so cheerful when I'm killing them? They sing to me and talk to me, which they never used to do before Joseph got me on to drinking them. Why do they like me at all? And why like me now that I'm drinking them? Maybe they all hate each

146

other and are happy to see each other die. Maybe they don't die. Maybe my stomach is full of the life-essence of coffee beans. I might be crawling with these parasites, all the way down my throat and through my insides, lined with boiled chatterboxes. I crossed my legs at the thought of living pee. Maybe the sewers are alive, a big talking soup just lying there under my feet on the pavement. Unless they've got some plan to infect the whole world with coffee, how can they be happy about that?

Misery set in; I needed consolation. I put the cup to my lips, and the sweet froth kissed me back. Hot black caffeine set about sweeping my head out, while the beans were singing *Keep Your Sunny Side Up* in four-part harmony. I listened, and gave them a brief round of applause at the end – well, I tapped my now-empty cup a couple of times, anyway.

"Time to get dressed, meet the day," said the beans. I sighed, showered, and dressed, in that order, then stood in front of the mirror, trying to do something with my flat-like-my-life hair. "You look like a million dollars!" the beans lied at the tops of their voices. I scowled, shut them in a cupboard, and headed out. I didn't forget my bus pass, either.

It was while I was typesetting at my keyboard – I am an assistant, and a good one, and woe betide anyone who says the S-word – that the matter clarified. I would get a dog, I badly needed one, and I knew exactly where. That'd show Joseph, damn him.

My boss interrupted my scheming: "Genevieve, a cup of coffee if you don't mind." My keyboard threw me a look of sympathy.

"Of course not, it's what I'm here for." I trilled, and skipped off to the shoebox-that-has-the-nerve-to-call-itself-a-kitchen, biting my bootlicking tongue all the way. "Kitchen." I said to the peach-tiled walls. "Call yourself a kitchen? Useless. Absobloodylutely useless. Right. Coffee."

There was a jar of instant in the cupboard. "Do you really think being a good secretary leads to promotion?" they mumbled as I unscrewed the cap. Being instant, they mumbled and had an irritating accent. They didn't know a damn thing about office politics either.

"Shut up," I told them. "And don't call me a secretary. I'm just going to make coffee with you."

"It's what we're here for," they murmured.

"Death!" I said. "Anyway, I'm on to you, you and your conspiracy. When I leave this afternoon, I'm going to get me a dog, and then I'll have you covered."

"You can never cover everything," came the world-weary rustle from the jar. "It's people like your boss who have control." I took control of the kettle and switched it on in preparation for boiling the little cinders. Maybe instants would be easier to kill.

"I'm going to the pet-shop, and guess who works there?" I said to them.

"Tell us," they muttered.

"Oh, you are so inferior! *My* beans would at least *sound* interested. But I'll tell you who works there, that crop-headed hippy Joseph dumped me for works there. God, the humiliation, he actually dropped me for a vegetarian!"

"Men were born to go wandering," the instants sighed.

"Talking to yourself, Genevieve?" said Sally, coming into the shoebox.

"Do you have to make coffee too?" I asked her, wearing my sympathetic grin.

"No, His Nibs wants tea," she said, fetching it from a lower cupboard, and giving the door a kick with her elegant leg to close it. "*Were* you talking to yourself? You weren't were you?"

"There's a new thing of milk in the fridge," I sidetracked.

"Thanks, but seriously, who were you talking to? You haven't got yourself a mobile, have you?"

"As if," I shrugged in my modesty.

"So, who were you talking to?" Nosy bint. Three perfectly good evasions and she's still at me.

"The coffee," I confessed; I couldn't say I'd been talking to myself. "They think I'll get promoted if I bootlick enough."

"What other chances have you got?" muttered the instants, while Sally said "Well, we can dream, I suppose." The kettle clicked off and I thought about kicking her.

"Life needs dreams," whispered the grounds. Sally ignored them. I took a spoon and dropped some of them into a cup, and sealed the others off in their jar. Sally got to the kettle before me and doused her tea-bag – tea bags never have any personality, it must be the grey bag those shredded little leaves are in, maybe I'd get more conversation out of tea-leaves – so I had to stand and wait by the stained old cup. She splashed in milk and skipped out with a "See ya."

"She'll be promoted before me," I complained to the instants in the mug. "I can't even beat her to a kettle."

They weren't listening, but kept whispering, "Life needs dreams, life needs dreams." I lifted the kettle and poured a stream of steaming water into the cup, drowning them.

I bowed and scraped my way through the rest of the day; I sat at my keyboard, which sympathised as I thought about Joseph, damn him. Damn his green eyes and supple back and public-school smile, and damn his good taste in jumpers and damn the freesias he used to bring me, damn the cappuccino he'd introduced me to and all those lessons in coffee-bean connoisseurship, and double damn him in particular for saying we needed space from each other. He could at least have said something original. And then, I told my keyboard – well, I didn't tell it out loud because silence was required in the office, but I gave it a reproachful look and it seemed to understand – he took up with that short-nailed vegetarian from the local petshop. The bastard didn't even like pets.

Thus I whiled away the time, talking to my keyboard: by recent standards, a typical day. However, I managed to survive until I managed to escape, and I made it on to the bus without leaving my bus pass at the office. Today, I reflected, might be a good day after all.

It wasn't far from the bus stop to the pet shop. There was a big window on either side of the door, and in each was a nest of puppies. I tapped at a window full of scuffling black scotties. "Hello puppies," I said. "Fancy a job?" There were a few little yaps, but none of them answered. Clearly, they couldn't hear through the glass. I tried the other window, full of spaniels of some sort. "Hello, dogs," I said. "Can you hear me, or am I talking to myself?"

I was talking to myself. Time to go in.

The door gave an annoying electronic beep as I walked in. I frowned at it, but it wasn't repentant: it repeated the beep as it swung shut. I took a quick glance around. There were two attendants, a woman with blue and black dreadlocks and a man with specs, both in the red T-shirt with the shop's logo on it. Neither of them was Sukie. They threw some helpful glances my way, but I was more in the mood for lurking, so I ducked my head and examined some fake bones on the shelf, lying dusty and hangdog with nothing to say for themselves. I'd need a collar, a lead, a basket, some dog food and, of course, a dog. A male, I think, so he can keep me company; get a nice male dog and have him neutered. I'll enjoy that. And where was Sukie today? I sauntered to the back of the shop and looked at the glowing fish. The swanned around their green lit-up boxes, round-eyed and serene like little Buddhists. A perfect world, they live in, I reflected – weeds and water, air bubbles and clean gravel, and they all like each other equally. And they're not very clever, either – who could ask for more? Maybe I'll come back here if I ever need a guru.

"Can I help you?" said a voice in my ear. It was the blue-headed woman. I put on my honest smile.

"Oh, yes please, I was just woolgathering here. The fact is, I'm looking to buy a dog."

"One of the ones in the window? The Scotties or the Cocker Spaniels?" she said.

"The spaniels," I said. I want no truck with a dog named after a country; times are volatile enough.

"Have you ever owned a dog before?"

"Well, not for years," I lied, never having owned any pet, unless you count coffee beans. "But we had spaniels when I was growing up, and I've kind of got to missing them, you know?"

"So you know about exercising them and so on…" she questionnaired.

"Well yes. And my house isn't huge, but there's a garden and it's near the common, it's the same house I grew up in" – this is true, my only inheritance – "and our dogs always did fine in it."

"Yes, I'm sure that sounds fine," she said, looking a little surprised – I must have been sounding irritable. I smiled again.

"How much are the spaniels?"

151

"They're two hundred and ninety-five pounds," she told me. Plus leads and baskets, well, that's me on short rations for a month. But still, it's not like I have anyone to go clubbing or dining with, I sighed. Think of it as an investment, something to talk to on lonely evenings.

"That sounds just fine," I sparkled at her. "Can I have a talk to them and see which one I get on with?" She smiled and went back to the till, and I hung myself over the partition into the window, to talk to them.

"Hello dogs," I said. "Which of you is ready to work for me?" They squirmed over each other and started a short, fat canine pyramid to climb up to me, heaped up like – well, like a packet of furry coffee beans. They were wet-eyed and hopeful, though, rather than smug. "I believe," I said, "that we shall get on very well. You see, what I need is a translator. Who here thinks they have what it takes, eh?" I put my hand in the box and unpiled them, dispensing them into a troupe of wagging tails. "Stand still," I told them, "I need to pick one of you. Darn it, why does everything in my life that's supposed to help me pile up in packs?"

At that moment, one particularly lop-eared moppet gave a warning yip and pointed over my shoulder. I glanced up and saw, reflected in the window in front of us, the lissome, slowly-advancing form of Sukie. "I'll have you," I told him: plainly he was on my side. I picked him up and cuddled him, and then whipped round sharp as a snake to face her.

She was advancing on tiptoe, staring as if she couldn't believe it. "Hello Sukie," I said.

"Genevieve?" Well, who else? My puppy gave me a supportive lick. "What are you doing here?"

"I'm buying a puppy," I told her.

"Genevieve –" She sounded nervous.

"Don't think I'm spying," I said. "I have no interest in

you; however, I do want to buy a dog, to comfort me in my loneliness."

"Genevieve –" She was sounding defensive now.

"Surely you wouldn't deny me the consolation?" She bit her lip. *Not very tough, is she?* the puppy whispered in my ear.

She was looking beautiful as ever, her pixie face rosy, her soft, spiky hair shining, her flat-chested-but-slim-and-graceful body much as it always was. "It's quite all right," I told her. "I really do just want to buy a puppy."

"Why buy it here?" she said, her voice tense.

"Oh come now Sukie; if I just wanted to bother you I'd hardly buy a dog, would I? I'd buy some fish food. Honestly, you'd think the world revolved around you the way you carry on. Would you rather I'd gone somewhere else?"

She chewed her lip some more. Obviously she would, but she couldn't say so, certainly not without losing that guileless femininity which Joseph found so captivating after all my carping. "Well, I'd love to oblige, but this little dog and I have already made friends, so I'd hate to break his heart and abandon him here." The dog gave me another lick, bless his scrabbly paws. "See? He loves me. You can't just abandon someone who loves you, now can you? It wouldn't be fair, heaven only knows what it would do to them."

"For godsake, Genevieve, why can't you just deal with your life like the rest of us?" she snapped.

"Who's the royal we?" I asked; aha, there's a crack in the lacquer after all. The sweet face had a scowl on it: a great improvement.

"Everyone. You think you're the only one who's ever had to put up with things?"

The puppy whimpered as my fingers clenched in his fur.

Joseph must have been talking about me. He's turned against me, he's encouraging her to scorn me. I'm going to send that guy a letter-bomb, I swear it. "Far from it. I'm sure there's plenty of people who have to deal with you. Thousands. Who knows, maybe someday these little pets may rise against you. An army of budgies to peck the nose off your pretty face; I could have a word with them about it if you like. I want to buy my dog first, though – what happened to the customer being always right?"

"I'll get you someone else," she muttered, and hurried off to the back of the shop, her neat, heart-shaped bottom swinging in distress.

I hugged the puppy. "You're a darling, aren't you?" I whispered to him. "What shall I call you?"

The puppy was a great success when I got him home. I still hadn't thought of a name for him, and he'd made no suggestions, but he scampered through my door with a great show of enthusiasm.

I took him up to my bedroom to make introductions. The beans were chanting for me: "Welcome home! Welcome home!" The dog gave a yip.

"I have got a dog," I informed the beans.

"A woman's best friend," they enthused.

"And what's more, he's going to help me, I'm on to the conspiracy you have and he's going to be my translator. I'll show you."

"We have no secrets, we are an open book," the blameless little beans affirmed.

"Ha!" I said. "I'm going to find out what your ground up cousins say!"

I waited for the platitude.

None came.

"My God," I said. "That shut you up! You really are up

to something!"

"Not in the least," the beans told me. "There just didn't seem to be a sensible answer."

"I doubt you," I muttered.

The puppy gave another yip. "Cutchie coo," said the beans. The puppy whined. I picked him up and sat down.

"Now listen," I said to him. "We're going to work things out. I shall feed you, shelter you, and be nice to you. In return, you will become housebroken, and will act as a translator when necessary; you will also refrain from going off with other women, unlike some people we could name. Do we have a deal?" The puppy whined, licked me, then bit me on the nose.

"Stop it!" I said. "No biting. Bad dog. Only people are allowed to bite me, and then only if they're tall and handsome, not small and fuzzy like you. Bad dog." I gave him a little shake. He whimpered, and put his tail between his legs.

"That's the way!" said the beans. "Don't let him get away with it."

The puppy whimpered again, and cast me a sorrowful look. "Now don't go trying to break my heart," I told him. Round wet eyes gazed at me, and a little tongue flicked out.

"Heartbreaker," said the beans, and a little crack appeared in my heart.

"Sorry doggy," I said, and gave him a hug. "Peace?" He stopped whimpering, and started wriggling instead. "Is that a yes or a no? Ow, mind your claws! Oh, all right, down you get." He scampered off, and tried to bite my curtains. I kicked off my shoes. My feet thanked me. "Valentino. That's what I'll call you," I told him. "A good name for a heartbreaker. You don't look like a Valentino, of course, but it can't be helped. And anyway, you're the only valentine I'm going to get this year."

"Nonsense!" said the beans. "An attractive woman like you? Chin up!"

"Your faith in me is touching," I said. "How about if I drink some of you?"

"Get it while you're young," said the beans – or at least most of them did.

"Valentino!" I called. "Here, boy…" I whistled. He looked round. "Come on boy, here… Oh do me a favour, eh?" He wagged his tail. "Oh, well," I said, and went over to scoop him up. "Now listen," I whispered to him. "I want you to tell me what those ground up beans are saying." He gave me an innocent look, and didn't say anything. The strong silent type, plainly, but a type that understands.

I put him down by the cappuccino set-up. "A nice bowl of water for you, and a cappuccino for me," I said, pouring out a bowl. He buried his nose in it, his tongue furling in and out of his mouth. The beans were singing again: *You'd Be So Nice To Come Home To*.

"Are you mocking me?" I asked them. They kept on singing, so I poured some of them into the grinder. That'd interfere with their perfect pitch. Some nice squeaky notes would do nicely, cheeky little schemers. "Okay, Valentino," I whispered. "Now this is it. They'll go squeaky so I can't hear them, then you do your stuff." I switched on the grinder.

For a frozen instant, Valentino did nothing. Then he exploded, barking like a wild mad thing and tearing around the room. The beans were getting sharper and sharper and rose quickly out of my hearing. "What are they saying Valentino?" I yelled over the noise, but Valentino was crouched down, shaking his head and scuffling. "Valentino?" I turned to switch off the grinder and remove the grounds, and when I looked back, he was still crouched down, shaking and cowering in a corner.

"Valentino? What's the matter?" The puppy whined, and a puddle appeared on the floor at his feet. "Oh God," I muttered, and picked up yesterday's newspaper, still on the floor, to mop it up. "What's with you?"

Valentino looked at me, his head and tail ducked between his little legs, and put another crack in my heart.

"Was it the noise? Was that it?" I asked him. "Oh, poor baby. Don't worry, it was just a big noise, nothing scary. Poor little Valentino." I stroked his soft head, crooning to him. "Poor Tino. Don't worry, just a big noise."

"Chicken," said the coffee beans.

"Shut up," I said. "He's only little."

I did finally manage to get my cappuccino made, by the method of putting Tino in another room while the machine was on. Over a fluffy, delicious cup of cappuccino and a bowl of puppy biscuits, we discussed living arrangements.

"This is Friday," I told him. "So I have the Bank Holiday weekend to settle you in. After that, I go back to work. Now tell me honestly, if I left you alone in the house all day, could I trust you?" Valentino ate a biscuit doubtfully. "Thought not. So what shall we do?"

He wagged his tail. "How about this?" I said. "I'll re-schedule my work hours, take a longer lunch break and come visit you then make the hours up in the evening. And you can stay in the kitchen and garden with the radio on while I'm gone, where the beans won't hassle you. Like that idea?"

Valentino came and sat on my foot, and wagged his tail in agreement. I picked him up and stroked him.

"You're getting domestic," warned the beans.

"Hmm," I said. "Drink you or not, I still don't trust you. Once I've got him less scared of noises, you and I are going to have words."

At that point the doorbell rang. "Fresh excitement!" cried the beans, their good humour restored. "Take on the world!"

I opened my window and leaned out over the street. When I saw who was at my door, I nearly fell out of the window. It was Joseph.

"What are you doing here?" I said.

Joseph looked to and fro, plainly wondering where the voice came from. "Joseph…" A pleasing look of confusion settled on his face. "Joseph…" I wonder how long I can stretch this out?

Valentino barked. "I'm not being a sadist," I whispered to him. "I just think a little confusion won't do him any harm." Tino barked again. Joseph was looking to and fro, getting restless, and the awful thought struck me that he might leave. "Joseph, I'm up here! Up, look up! What do you want?"

Joseph looked up. To my dismay, his eyes were as green as ever, his skin as clear; he was wearing a tasteful hand-made jumper that I'd always liked on him, that I used to borrow when we went out walking too late and cold set in. I had to be thankful for small mercies, I supposed, because his face was furious. If he hadn't looked so angry, I might have thrown myself at his feet.

"Genevieve, what the hell are you playing at?" he demanded.

"What's wrong? I often lean out of the window instead of answer the door."

"Go on, stick up for yourself," whispered the coffee beans.

"No, Gen, you know what I'm talking about," said Joseph.

"Oh, it's Gen now is it? You haven't called me Gen for

months."

"Damn it, Gen, answer me. What were you thinking of?"

He never sounded this angry when we were splitting up. "I honestly don't know what you're talking about, so if you'd care to explain, then we lesser morsels might stand a chance of answering you."

"Are you going to let me in?" He always hated scenes in public.

"Not till you tell me what you're on about." Valentino came and nestled round my ankles, my beans rallied in support.

"I'm talking about you going to the shop and harassing Sukie, that's what I'm talking about."

"Well, if that's what you're talking about," I told him sweetly, "then I don't think I'm going to let you in."

"Sukie was crying when I got home, Genevieve." He glanced about the street; no-one was within earshot, so he started up again. "You upset her for no reason, it was just spite."

"No reason? I bought a puppy," I said, and picked Valentino up. "Look, here he is. Isn't he sweet?"

"Damn it, you can't just buy an animal to upset someone! You need your head seen to."

"I didn't!" I shouted down. "I wanted to buy a dog." Valentino yelped, and I loosened my grip on him.

"*Why?*" he demanded in an end-of-the-tether voice I'd never heard before.

"Something to sleep with, something faithful…" Joseph gave my front door a bang with his fist. I put Tino on the floor and leaned out further. "And if it reassures you, I did have a genuine reason for buying him, I only thought of going to the shop after I decided I wanted a dog."

"So you did go there on purpose."

"Yes of course I did, but I did have a reason, it wasn't just to plague you. That was just a sideline."

"Why?" He looked tired.

"To translate my coffee grounds."

"Gen, for God's sake – "

"No, no, I needed him. When I grind them up their voices go too high for me to hear and I need to know if they mind being ground up and drunk, and I can't ask them." Joseph stared up at me shouting, his handsome face bewildered. "So I needed a dog, dogs hear higher than people, I needed a dog to translate what they were saying."

"*What?*"

"Because I always want coffee these days, all the time, and if I can have what I want then I can get on with my life. If I can just have little things like coffee and flowers." I found I wasn't shouting any more. "But if it hurts flowers to pick them or coffee to drink them, then it might be too much for a small pleasure. Joseph, you gave me this coffee habit, and I want to know if it's worth keeping."

"Genevieve, nobody's – "

"Or if it does hurt the beans, then I need to know if I care. Or if the beans don't die when you drink them, then where do they go? In me, in the sewers? I don't want there to be talking beans wherever I go, it could be very dangerous. I want to know if you did a bad thing to give me this coffee habit."

"Gen – " said Joseph. "Gen, what's wrong with you?"

"*Why shouldn't I have a dog?*" I shrieked.

"Gen, I think you need help," said Joseph.

Valentino struggled, and I set him down. "I don't need help from you," I said. "Get away from my front door."

"Stand up for yourself!" said the coffee beans. I picked up the packet.

"Gen, I think maybe you should see a psychiatrist," said

160

Joseph, as I took aim.

"See one yourself!" I said, and threw a bean.

"Tally-ho!" it cried as it fell, landing with a little tap on his shoulder.

"Gen?"

I threw another. "Charge!" it shouted, hitting his head. "Take that! Get him!" shouted the beans in their packet. I threw a handful down at him.

"Take your fucking coffee back!" I said. Beans pattered around him.

"Gen, stop it!" Joseph shouted.

"Pennies from heaven," I said, scattering the brown little confetti, all yelling with martial ardour.

"*Genevieve!*"

Valentino barked, and put his paws up at the sill to look out. "See?" I whispered. "That's the bad man who gave me a coffee habit then gave me the push. Bark at him!"

Tino did bark. I will give him that much credit. Bark, he did, but he also wagged his tail, and this was the crux of the matter. "Tino!" I told him. "Show some loyalty!" Swish, swish, went the silk-fringed tail, to and fro and to and fro, and he barked a happy greeting to the man in the street, the funny man with coffee in his hair.

"And now what?" I said aloud, sitting on the floor with Tino beside me. Joseph was gone, gone back to pretty, sweet Sukie. Poor Sukie. She is quite sweet, really – anyway, she didn't make a fuss in the shop. She could have stopped them from selling me Tino, easily. I gave Tino a pat, and he licked my hand.

"Good riddance to him, eh?" said the beans.

"Who?"

"Joseph."

"I'm not sure," I said. "He said I needed a psychiatrist."

"Nonsense," they declared.

"Of course it's nonsense," I said, "but why would I have wanted a man who thought I was crazy?"

"Atta girl," they said. Tino licked my hand again, and put his head on my knee. He didn't agree.

"Why were you wagging at him?" I asked. "You're supposed to be on my side." Tino heaved a sigh.

"Tino," I said, "do you fancy doing some translation? I know you're scared of the noise…"

I scooped him up, dropped him outside the door, ground some beans, and brought him back. "Okay, Tino," I said. "Now what are they saying?"

Tino whimpered, sniffed them, then came and put his head back on my lap.

They say, he was telling me, *that you drink too much coffee.*

This morning, as on many mornings, the coffee bean said to me, "Rise and shine."

"Oof," I said, sitting up. "Morning, Tino." Tino jumped out his basket and fetched his lead.

"Let me get dressed first," I said. "Then we'll have a run on the common, then breakfast." He put his head on the floor, wanting to play, but he's over a year old now, he can wait.

I showered, whistling to myself. The adjusted hours had been a good idea. Or at least, good for my poor bitten tongue: I'd had to stop bootlicking in order to persuade my boss to allow them.

I dried myself and went back to my room to dress and brush my hair. "Nice haircut," said the coffee bean, the single bean I keep as a souvenir. I prefer tea these days anyway.

"Thanks," I said. "I like it." The bean, I've noticed, has

162

been much less strident since I threw its compatriots away. It knows its place, I guess. Certainly it never tries to get out of the cupboard.

Later that day I went to make coffee and tea in the still-very-small kitchen. I unscrewed the coffee jar – still instant, I must do something about that. There's a promotion round coming up, so I'm going to show initiative and team spirit: maybe I'll bring in my cappuccino maker. It's just gathering dust at home.

"Good morning, coffee," I said to the contents of the jar.

"What's good about it?" they muttered.

"Oh, hush. There's to be no whining in this kitchen. I'm just going to brew you, and if you don't like that, then that's just too bad."

"Aren't we the tough lady these days?" said the instants bitterly.

"Oh, you don't like that? Sorry, but you'll just have to lump it. I'm not hooked on caffeine any more, so you can have no possible influence over me. Anyway, I'm bigger than you. So behave."

"Talking to coffee, Genevieve?" said Sally, coming in to make tea.

"Of course," I said. "I just don't drink it. It's bad for you."

KATHARINE WHITFIELD

Notes on Contributors

Richard Antwi is a second generation Ghanaian, one of six children. He grew up on an inner city estate in London and was the first in his family to go to university. He played county football until he was sixteen and played in a sound system until he was seventeen. A few of his contemporaries went on to be pop stars, DJs and Premiership football players. Richard decided to go to university and battled against peer group pressure, stereotypes and other obstacles to get there.

His interests include music, new technology and business. He founded a company at university which promotes music on behalf of major record companies. Richard recently won an award from Andersen Consulting for his writing on the convergence of new technologies. He is currently working on his first novel which deals with the problems of identity from the perspective of second generation black people in England.

Richard is 21 years old and is reading Law at Lincoln College, Oxford.

Jay Basu was born in London, and still lives there.

Heather Clark is a DPhil student at Lincoln College, Oxford, where she is focusing on contemporary Irish poetry. She did her BA at Harvard and her MPhil in Anglo-Irish Literature at Trinity College, Dublin. She has also written for *Let's Go Travel Guides* in Ireland. This year she was awarded the Martin Starkie Prize for Poetry at Oxford.

Katharine Edgar was born in Maldon, Essex in 1972, and educated at Chelmsford County High School. She read

Classics at St John's College, Oxford followed by an MA in Museum Studies at Leicester. Currently she is at Newnham College, Cambridge working on a PhD on the nineteenth century traveller and collector Edward Daniel Clarke.

Laura James is in her final year at Magdalen College, Oxford, studying PPE – a discipline which manifestly unfits her for writing anything longer than a postcard. She was brought up in Kenya, and has since travelled widely in the vain hope of regaining some of that early glamour. Her hobby is the translation of Latin poetry. Nobody knows why.

Anna Khoo is a second year medic at Sidney Sussex, Cambridge, and has two scars on her right knee. She would like to thank Mrs Perkins for her cooperation.

David McCallam 31 years old, originally from Cockermouth in the Lake District, married to Rachel with a 10-month-old daughter, Eve. I have studied previously in London and Warwick and am now completing a PhD in 18th century French literature (circa the Revolution). I have lived and worked in both France and Hungary before, mainly pimping the mother tongue abroad. I recently returned to Budapest to do a marathon, a feat requiring great physical stamina and a greater lack of imagination. Qualities also needed to eat locally.

Hillary Stevens was born and grew up in San Antonio, Texas. In 1998 she received a BA in Classics from Harvard University. She is currently working towards an MSc in Social Anthropology at Linacre College, Oxford.

Katharine Whitfield is a third-year English student at Christ's College, Cambridge; she is twenty-one years old. This is her third appearance in the *Anthologies*. She doesn't drink coffee and hates dogs. Next year she plans to take a Creative Writing MA at the University of East Anglia.